Treats and

Crime

Whiskers in the Winery

M.R. Diaz

Contents

Introduction

Amidst the allure of Whistlewood's vineyards, a sabotage awaits; as two hearts entwine deeper, can love ferment amidst a mystery as old as wine?

In the charming town of Whistlewood, as preparations for the annual Wine and Whimsy event brew, Sophie and Oliver—a blossoming couple—find themselves amidst a winery sabotage. With their pets, Thor and Luna, they must uncork old rivalries and bitter histories to save the event. Amidst wine barrels and starlit proposals, this cozy mystery serves love, intrigue, and a taste of Whistlewood's rich legacy in one intoxicating pour

The Wine and Whimsy Whirlwind

Sophie Clarke brushed a loose strand of hair away from her face, her fingers leaving a faint streak of soil on her forehead. She beamed as she gently placed a chrysanthemum into its designated spot within a rustic flower arrangement. The scent of fresh flowers mingled with the earthy aroma of potting soil, filling the air of her cozy little florist shop, Blooms & Blossoms.

A quaint bell chimed, signaling a visitor. Sophie looked up and her eyes instantly brightened, recognizing the man walking through the door.

"Oliver! What brings you here?" she asked, her voice imbued with genuine delight.

Oliver Montgomery, owner of Whistlewood's one and only bookstore, Montgomery's Mysterious Tomes, smiled as he crossed the threshold. His eyes—always soft, warm, and inviting—locked onto Sophie's.

"I thought I'd come by and see how the flower queen of Whistlewood was faring," Oliver said, holding up a reusable tote bag. "And I brought some fresh copies of wine-making literature for the Wine and Whimsy event."

Sophie's face lit up. "Oh, how delightful! This town's going to need all the whimsy it can get, considering the vineyard disaster."

As Oliver approached the counter, his eyes couldn't help but wander around the floral haven. Glass jars filled with color, rustic flower pots, and sprigs of baby's breath adorned the wooden shelves. The whole place was a refreshing contrast to his world of ink and parchment, yet it felt equally enchanting.

Sophie, taking the tote bag from him, eagerly flipped through the books. "Ah, 'The Elixir of Life: A Tale of Grapes and Wine.' Perfect! This will be the star of my special flower-wine table arrangement."

"Flower-wine table arrangement? That sounds fascinating. Do tell," Oliver inquired, intrigued by Sophie's never-ending pool of creativity.

"Well," Sophie began, her eyes twinkling like morning dew on a fresh rose petal, "I'm experimenting with flower-infused wines. Lavender Moscato, Rose Rosé, you name it. I'm even working on a Chrysanthemum Chardonnay."

"Absolutely mesmerizing," Oliver said, visibly impressed. "You're going to steal the show."

Sophie smiled but sighed, her eyes clouding with a momentary gloom. "I just hope it's enough to lift everyone's spirits, especially after the vineyard sabotage."

Oliver sensed the heaviness settling in and reached for her hand. "Sophie, if there's one thing I've learned, it's that you have an incredible talent for bringing joy when it's needed the most. You're like a sunflower in a field of... well, not sunflowers."

Sophie chuckled. "Quite the poetic analogy, Mr. Montgomery."

The two shared a warm smile, their hands still interlocked. Yet, behind their eyes loomed the unspoken anxiety about the upcoming event. How could it be a success with the town's prized wine supply jeopardized?

, a distant wail of a siren pierced through the cozy atmosphere. Sophie and Oliver looked at each other, sensing that Whistlewood's calm was about to be disrupted once more.

"I have a feeling," Oliver said softly, "that this Wine and Whimsy event will be more than just sipping Chardonnay and reading biographies."

Sophie nodded, her grip on Oliver's hand tightening. "I agree. But whatever it is, we'll face it together."

As Oliver left the store, both knew that the upcoming event would serve not just wine and whimsy, but also a mysterious adventure that neither could foresee.

And so began the tale of a curious sabotage that would uncork old rivalries, bitter grapes, and the rich, intoxicating history of Whistlewood's wine-making legacy.

The sun cast its golden hue over rows and rows of grapevines, painting a picture of tranquility that belied the undercurrent of tension gripping Whistlewood's most renowned vineyard, Vino Veritas. Sophie and Oliver, holding hands as they walked, felt the change in atmosphere as soon as they entered the property.

"Something's not right," Sophie murmured, her eyes scanning the vineyard workers who moved with a sense of urgency and whispered amongst themselves. "It's like there's a dark cloud over this place."

"You mean aside from the spoiled barrels?" Oliver quipped, but his attempt at humor fell flat. The weight of the sabotage was palpable.

They were greeted by Marianne, the vineyard manager, a middle-aged woman with a hardened face etched with lines of worry. "Ah, Sophie, Oliver, thank you for coming. Your support means a lot in these difficult times."

"We're all in this together, Marianne," Oliver assured her, squeezing Sophie's hand as if to emphasize the unity.

"Let's see if we can't add some floral magic and literary charm to lighten the mood, shall we?" Sophie added, mustering as much cheerfulness as she could.

Marianne led them to a grand wooden table where the event was to take place, surrounded by barrels and overlooking the sprawling vineyard. "Here we are. I thought this would be a perfect setting for your flower-wine arrangement and book exhibit, Sophie, Oliver."

"It's beautiful," Sophie breathed out, already envisioning how her floral creations would bring life to the setting.

"As it's going to be an evening event, how about adding some fairy lights and vintage candelabras?" Oliver suggested, his eyes lighting up with the image of a magical evening amid the grapevines.

Marianne smiled for the first time that day. "I think that would be absolutely lovely."

As Sophie and Oliver began discussing where to set up, they were interrupted by a frantic vineyard worker rushing up to Marianne. "Sorry to disturb you, but there's another problem. One of the reserve barrels— the seal's been tampered with!"

"What?!" Marianne exclaimed, her face blanching with new worry.

"I should go handle this. Please, excuse me," Marianne said, rushing off to attend to the latest crisis.

Sophie and Oliver exchanged a worried glance. The sense of impending chaos was escalating, and their efforts to lift spirits seemed like putting a band-aid on a gaping wound.

"Oliver, do you feel that?" Sophie asked, her voice tinged with desperation. "It's as if we're standing on the edge of something much larger and more sinister."

Before Oliver could respond, a mysterious note floated down from nowhere, landing on their setup table. Oliver picked it up and read aloud, "'To find the truth, follow the last light of the day.'"

Sophie's eyes met Oliver's. Both knew that this was more than just an event; it was the unfolding of a new Whistlewood mystery, one that had chosen them as its reluctant sleuths.

And as the sun dipped below the horizon, the last rays seemed to point towards the old, decrepit storage barn at the edge of the vineyard. A chill ran down their spines. Whistlewood was whispering its secrets, and it was up to them to listen.

As twilight settled over the vineyard, casting shadows that danced like restless spirits, Sophie and Oliver made their way back towards the main gathering area. They were interrupted by the sight of Gerald, the vineyard owner, a man of imposing stature with graying hair and usually sparkling eyes that today seemed dull and distracted.

"Gerald, are you all right?" Sophie inquired, concerned by his disheveled appearance. His suit was wrinkled, his tie askew, and he seemed to be muttering to himself.

"Hmm? Oh, Sophie, Oliver, didn't see you there," Gerald replied, attempting to put on a smile that didn't quite reach his eyes.

"You seem preoccupied," Oliver observed. "Is everything okay, considering, well, all that's happened?"

Gerald looked around nervously before leaning in and whispering, "To be honest, I'm not sure. It's not just the spoiled barrels; there are other strange happenings. Odd noises at night, barrels moved from their original places, and now this," he pulled out another mysterious note similar to the one Sophie and Oliver had found. It read, "The past always ferments, until uncorked."

Sophie and Oliver exchanged a meaningful glance. The mystery was deepening, and the sense of urgency was intensifying.

"Sounds like we've all been getting these mysterious messages," Oliver noted, sharing their own note with Gerald.

"This is most peculiar, and a bit frightening if I'm being honest," Gerald admitted. "I've put my heart and soul into this vineyard; it would kill me to see it fail because of some, some—"

"Saboteur?" Sophie offered.

"Precisely," Gerald confirmed, his voice tinged with bitterness. "I've always believed in the goodness of Whistlewood, but this makes me question everything."

Sophie looked at Oliver and back at Gerald. "We're in this together, Gerald. And we're going to get to the bottom of it. This event will go on, and it will be a success. Whistlewood deserves that."

"Thank you, both of you. But be careful; whoever is behind this is playing a dangerous game," Gerald warned, his eyes clouded with a mixture of gratitude and apprehension.

As Gerald walked away, Sophie and Oliver felt the gravity of their newfound mission. But it wasn't just the vineyard's reputation at stake; it was the soul of Whistlewood itself.

, Sophie's dog, Thor, and Oliver's cat, Luna, scampered into the clearing, playfully chasing one another until they reached their owners. As if sensing the tension, they both paused and looked up, their eyes reflecting a mixture of innocence and uncanny wisdom.

The couple knelt down to pet them, drawing comfort from their loyal companions. But as they stood back up, they caught sight of something—or someone—moving furtively near the old storage barn, momentarily illuminated by the rising moon.

"Heart and soul, was it?" Oliver whispered. " let's go find out who's trying to steal Whistlewood's."

Hand in hand, with their faithful pets by their side, they moved toward the barn. Each step took them closer to answers, but also deeper into a labyrinth of questions that seemed to echo Gerald's cryptic words: The past always ferments, until uncorked.

And as they reached for the barn door, a sudden gust of wind blew it open, as if inviting them into a story that was far from over.

Thor and Luna's Puzzling Paw-spects

In the leaf-dappled sunlight, the vineyard looked like a painter's idyllic fantasy, but to Thor and Luna, something felt oddly unsettling. As if they were paw-deep into a puzzle waiting to be solved.

Luna, the spirited Beagle with a keen nose, pranced along the edge of the vineyard's property, her senses tingling. She looked up at Thor, the wise grey cat perched on the fence, his eyes scrutinizing the comings and goings around the vineyard's main building. Something was amiss; both could sense it. The vineyard, usually bustling with activity, seemed quieter, almost tense.

"What do you think is happening, Thor?" Luna asked, her voice tinged with concern. She had an innate ability to sense when things were out of balance, a quality Thor admired.

"I'm not certain," Thor replied cautiously, his green eyes narrowed. "But have you noticed how the vineyard owner, Gerald, has been acting peculiar? He's usually so cheerful, especially right before the annual Wine and Whimsy event."

"You're right," Luna nodded. "He didn't even pet me the last time we saw him, and he always does! Also, there's a strange smell in the air; not the grapes or the soil, something... off."

Thor hopped down from the fence, landing gracefully next to Luna. "Perhaps we should do a bit of our own snooping around. This is our town too, and if something's wrong, we should know about it."

Luna wagged her tail, excited at the prospect of an adventure, especially one that had the potential to put things right. "Where should we start?"

Thor pondered for a moment before suggesting, "Let's begin by checking the storage sheds. They're usually off-limits, but I've seen Gerald heading there more frequently."

"A clandestine mission, how exciting!" Luna said, her ears perking up. "Are you ready?"

"As ready as I'll ever be," Thor replied, his tail flicking with anticipation.

The two pets shared a look of determination, aware that they were stepping into a world of unknowns. Yet, their loyalty to their humans and their community compelled them to dig deeper. With that, they trotted off, blending into the shadows, prepared for whatever lay ahead.

Thor's paws danced with anticipation as he led Luna through the labyrinth of grapevines, each sniff and paw-step a clandestine maneuver. They had to be stealthy; Gerald, the vineyard owner, and his crew could spot them at any moment, which would jeopardize their amateur but dedicated investigation. Luna followed with the grace of a seasoned acrobat, her agile body weaving through the narrow gaps between vines.

The sun was setting, casting a golden glow on the vineyard, but for Thor and Luna, it felt more like the stage lights of a theater. A theater where they were both the audience and the actors, and the drama was unfolding in real-time.

"Remember, no barking," Luna reminded Thor as they approached the area where they had seen the strange shadow earlier.

Thor wagged his tail in acknowledgment, his ears keenly alert for any sound out of the ordinary. Both animals paused as they reached the epicenter of the unusual activities, their senses working in overdrive. Luna's ears twitched as she picked up the sound of hushed voices coming from a small wooden shed near the far edge of the vineyard.

With a silent nod to each other, they inched closer, their hearts pounding in tandem. Thor could smell it more clearly now—the same foul scent he'd detected earlier, stronger this time. Luna's eyes widened as they approached the shed; the door was ajar, and she could see mysterious vials and tools scattered on a makeshift table inside.

Suddenly, a door creaked open in the distance. Gerald and another man stepped out of the main winery building, engaged in a hushed but heated discussion. Luna and Thor ducked behind a row of barrels, peering through the narrow gaps. They watched as Gerald handed the man an envelope. The man glanced inside, nodded, and quickly disappeared into the fading twilight.

"What was that all about?" Thor wondered silently, looking at Luna for answers.

Luna's eyes met his, filled with a mixture of fear and determination. "I don't know, but I have a feeling that whatever is going on here is bigger than a few spoiled barrels of wine."

, Thor's ears perked up again. A soft, eerie melody floated through the air, like a ghostly lullaby. It came from the direction of the shed.

"Did you hear that?" Luna whispered.

"Yes," Thor's eyes narrowed. "It's coming from where those mysterious vials are. What do you say, partner? Time to take a closer look?"

Luna nodded, and they darted toward the shed, hearts pounding but spirits unbreakable. Just as they reached the door, it swung open from the inside, as if pushed by an invisible force. They froze, their fur standing on end.

"Quick, hide!" Luna motioned to a pile of hay beside the shed. They dove into it just in time as a figure emerged from the shed, shrouded in darkness.

It was a race against time, and Thor and Luna were now more committed than ever to solve the mystery. With the night as their cover and their senses as their guide, they knew they were on the brink of a discovery.

Luna's nose twitched as the strong, unpleasant aroma grew stronger. It was a scent distinctly different from the fragrant bouquet of a well-aged wine—this was the smell of spoilage, of something rotten. Thor sensed it too; his whiskers quivered with unease.

The duo slipped out of their hay bale hiding spot, tails low, eyes sharp. The figure who had emerged from the shed was now nowhere to be seen, which was both a relief and an added layer of mystery. Thor gestured with a tilt of his head, indicating that they should head towards the source of the odor. Luna nodded, her ears perked in high alert. They moved with caution, each rustle of their paws muffled by the damp earth.

Thor's eyes widened as they reached a secluded part of the vineyard, far from the prying eyes of humans. What lay before them was astonishing: a pile of wooden barrels, each marked with the emblem of the vineyard, stacked haphazardly as though hastily hidden. Luna approached one of the barrels and sniffed; her nose recoiled instantly. This was the source of the smell, there was no doubt.

"What have they done?" Thor whispered, his eyes narrowed. "These are barrels of high-quality wine, meant for the festival. Why spoil them? And who is behind this?"

Luna's eyes darted around, thinking through their next moves. As she did, her gaze fell on a piece of torn fabric hanging from a protruding nail on one of the barrels. It was a subtle but telling clue. She barked softly to get Thor's attention and pointed to it with her paw.

Thor's eyes lit up. "Good catch, Luna! This could be a clue as to who is behind this. We need to show this to Sophie and Oliver."

Just as they prepared to take the fabric, a voice echoed through the vineyard, breaking the stillness of the evening. "Who's there? Show yourself!" It was Gerald, the vineyard owner, and he was heading in their direction.

Luna's eyes met Thor's in a moment of urgency. "Run!" Thor hissed, and they bolted, the torn fabric clenched in Luna's mouth.

As they dashed through the rows of grapevines, hearts pounding, they knew they had stumbled upon something far darker than they could have ever imagined. But who could be behind it, and why? These were questions that loomed large as they made their escape, the voice of Gerald growing fainter behind them.

Once they were at a safe distance, they paused, panting and exhilarated. Luna passed the torn fabric to Thor, who held it in his mouth with a sense of triumph.

"This is bigger than us," Thor said, his eyes serious but proud. "But we're one step closer to solving it."

"And to think," Luna added, her tail wagging despite the gravity of the situation, "this is just the beginning."

Sour Grapes and Sweeter Moments

Sophie Clarke, Whistlewood's go-to florist with an infectious smile, hummed a soft tune as she gracefully navigated her cozy flower shop. Today was a particularly special day, as she was fusing her expertise in florals with a newfound interest in winemaking. She was experimenting with flower-infused wines for the upcoming Wine and Whimsy event. The scent of roses, lavender, and fresh soil mingled with the heady aroma of fermenting grapes, filling the air with an intoxicating bouquet.

Next to her, a few bottles of white and red wines were lined up, ready to embrace the essence of her selected blooms. She picked up a rose petal, twirling it between her fingers before dropping it into a bottle of Chardonnay. A small smile danced across her lips as she envisioned guests at the event sipping this unique blend, captivated by its floral notes.

Her phone buzzed on the counter, and she saw Oliver's name flash on the screen. She picked it up eagerly, her face lighting up even more, if that was possible.

"Hey you," she greeted, "How's your day going?"

Oliver's warm voice came through the speaker. "It's going well. Just sorted out the last of the musician biographies for the event. How are your wine experiments coming along?"

Sophie glanced at her flower-infused creations. "It's still a work in progress, but I'm hopeful. Lavender Pinot Noir and Rose Chardonnay are just the beginning!"

Oliver chuckled, "Only you could make wine sound even more poetic. I can't wait to try them."

As she placed the phone back down, a small pang of worry pinched her. What if her floral wines weren't good enough? What if people didn't like them? Shaking off the thought, she told herself that innovation always came with risks. She looked at the infused wines, her little act of bravery in a bottle, and felt a surge of pride.

Sophie returned to her workstation, this time adding a sprinkle of dried violets to a Merlot, her thoughts drifting to Oliver. She imagined him reading poetry at the festival, taking a sip of her flower-infused wine. The thought alone gave her the confidence she needed. This was going to be special; she could feel it.

She placed a cork in the last bottle, sealing her adventurous spirit inside, unaware that outside her shop, Luna and Thor were onto an adventure of their own, one that could potentially affect the outcome of the Wine and Whimsy event.

Oliver Montgomery was engrossed in a thick tome about the history of winemaking. His quaint bookstore, a sanctuary of words and wisdom, had turned into a mini research hub for the upcoming Wine and Whimsy event. Amid the familiar scent of aged paper and ink, the fragrance of freshly brewed coffee wafted in from the attached café, melding seamlessly with his concentration.

He was reading up on the art and science of winemaking, eager to contribute his own brand of expertise to the festivities. He could already picture it: people sauntering in from the vineyard event, their palates tingling with Sophie's floral-infused wines, only to deepen their experience with the rich history of winemaking literature he'd provide.

His gaze moved to the empty chair opposite him, the one Sophie often occupied during her frequent visits to the bookstore. He visualized her sitting there, laughing at one of his jokes or engrossed in a floral design magazine. A sense of warmth enveloped him. In a town that seemed to have jumped out of a storybook, Sophie had become his favorite chapter.

His phone buzzed, pulling him from his thoughts. It was a message from Mrs. Harrington, one of the esteemed socialites of Whistlewood. "Oliver, do you think you could give a short talk on the history of wine during the event? People would love it!"

His heart leapt at the opportunity, not just to share knowledge but to impress Sophie. He quickly typed out a grateful acceptance.

Just as he was about to resume his reading, his eyes fell upon Baxter, his curious feline friend, who was peering intently out of the window. Oliver followed his gaze and saw Thor, the neighborhood's wise grey cat, and Luna, Sophie's playful Beagle, skirting around the corner, their faces filled with a purpose he couldn't quite comprehend.

Oliver shook his head with a chuckle. "What are you two up to?" he murmured to himself, his thoughts already threading through the intricacies of his upcoming talk and how Sophie might react to it.

Feeling a renewed sense of excitement, he marked a particularly enlightening passage in his book. Yes, this was the material that would not only educate but also entertain. He closed the book and took a deep, satisfied breath, unaware that his feline companion was contemplating mysteries that extended far beyond the pages of any book.

Sophie Clarke hummed a tune, her hands delicately arranging a cascade of vibrant roses into a vase. Her flower shop, blooming with colors and fragrances, mirrored her effervescent spirit. Each arrangement was more than a bouquet; it was a symphony of petals, leaves, and stems. Today, though, her creations were extra special. They were the muses for her upcoming floral-infused wines for the Wine and Whimsy event.

Just as she placed the last rose, she spotted Luna, her energetic Beagle, trotting in through the open back door. Luna paused to sniff a lavender bush before joining Sophie.

"Oh, Luna, I wish you could tell me about your little adventures," Sophie mused, scratching behind Luna's ears. The dog's tail wagged energetically, almost knocking over a flowerpot.

Sophie laughed and turned back to her workspace, her eyes landing on a small, cream-colored envelope nestled amid a pile of seed packets and floral design magazines. It was odd; she didn't remember seeing it before.

Curious, she tore open the envelope. Inside was a hand-written note:

"Are you sure your experiments should be shared with the town? Some things are better left bottled up."

Sophie's hands trembled, her heart pounding in her chest. She read the note again, half-expecting the words to change. They didn't. Someone was questioning her wine experiments, and the mysterious message drained the color from her world, making her roses seem less radiant.

Confused and slightly disoriented, she glanced around the shop, half-expecting to see a shadow lurking in some corner. Luna sensed her discomfort and gave a low growl, her eyes scanning the room.

Sophie took a deep breath, shaking off the unsettling feeling. "I won't let this spoil the event," she whispered to herself. Whoever sent the note had clearly never tasted her floral-infused wines; they could make even the sternest critics smile.

Determined, she grabbed her phone to call Oliver. She wanted to hear his comforting voice, to be wrapped in the warmth of his optimism. But just as she was about to dial, she hesitated. What if

Oliver started worrying? What if this soured his own enthusiasm for the event?

She set the phone down and stared at the note one last time before crumpling it into a ball and tossing it in the trash. This was her challenge to face, at least for now.

Sophie looked at Luna, her loyal friend and confidante. "We've got work to do, girl. We're not letting a piece of paper ruin our big day."

Yet, as she turned back to her flowers, the feeling that someone was watching her crept back, unsettling her once more. It was a mystery that went beyond the note, a story yet to be read, and it sent a shiver down her spine.

The Root of the Problem

Moonlight streamed through the cracks in the wooden boards that made up the vineyard cellar, casting shadows on the barrels and crates. Thor, the sleek grey cat, and Luna, the playful beagle, padded softly through the underground chamber. Their noses were twitching, picking up scents that were foreign to them—a blend of aged wood, earth, and something... mysterious.

Thor's green eyes flickered with a glint of curiosity as he leapt gracefully onto a wooden shelf. A row of old, dusty wine bottles caught his attention. The labels were faded, and the ink was smudged, but there was something compelling about them. Luna, feeling equally curious, stood on her hind legs, her front paws resting against the shelf as she sniffed the bottles.

"Look at this, Luna," Thor mewed softly, his paw gently tapping a bottle with an unusually intricate label. Luna wagged her tail and let out a quiet woof of agreement. This bottle was different; it practically radiated history.

The label was made of an old parchment, and its ink was not as faded as the others. It depicted a pair of entwined grapevines forming a heart, and below it, words written in an elegant, albeit weathered, cursive script. It was too dark to make out the words, but Luna's keen nose detected a blend of scents—grapes, of course, but also something floral. Lavender, perhaps?

Thor glanced at Luna, his eyes widening as if to say, "Should we?" Luna barked softly, her way of saying that some risks were worth taking. With utmost care, Thor used his agile paws to push the bottle toward the edge of the shelf. Luna positioned herself below, her mouth open, ready to catch it.

With a final nudge, the bottle tipped over the edge. Luna leapt, her jaws snapping shut around the bottle's neck an instant before it could crash to the floor. Success!

The duo carefully made their way back toward their hidden entrance, Luna carrying the mysterious bottle in her mouth. As they reached the earthen floor, Thor's paw brushed against another object. It was a notebook, old and weathered like the bottle. Thor nudged it open with his nose, revealing pages filled with handwritten notes and sketches of grapevines. Luna set the bottle down next to the notebook, her tail wagging furiously.

Just as Thor was about to paw through the notebook, a sudden noise echoed through the cellar—the sound of footsteps approaching. Thor's eyes met Luna's. Whoever was coming, it was likely they wouldn't appreciate the animals' late-night exploration. With no time to lose, Thor made a quick decision. He nudged the notebook back into its hiding spot but pushed a small piece of torn parchment under one of its pages—something Sophie and Oliver would surely notice. Luna picked up the bottle again in her mouth, and they dashed toward their exit, their hearts pounding in tandem.

As they squeezed through the narrow opening that led them back to the world above, Thor couldn't help but feel that they had just uncovered another layer in Whistlewood's rich tapestry of secrets. And as Luna carefully set down the mysterious bottle in a spot where Sophie and Oliver would find it, she let out a joyful bark, echoing Thor's sentiments exactly.

Neither of them could understand the words on that bottle or in that notebook, but they both knew they had found something significant, something that could hold the key to the town's—and perhaps their owners'—future.

As they retreated into the shadows, the cellar door creaked open. A beam of artificial light cut through the darkness, and a figure stepped in, pausing at the sight of the disturbed shelf. The adventure, it seemed, was far from over.

Thor and Luna, their hearts still racing from their narrow escape, couldn't resist the pull of another intriguing find. Luna's ears perked up as she caught a faint rustling sound coming from one of the walls. She pawed at a few loose bricks near a wine rack, sniffing intently. Thor joined her, his sharp feline senses also alert.

"What have you found?" Thor meowed, peering closely at the wall. With a yelp of excitement, Luna's paw nudged at a worn piece of paper wedged into a crack between two bricks. Intrigued, Thor extended a claw and gently hooked it onto the paper, pulling it free.

The paper was yellowed with age, and the ink had faded, but it was clearly a letter. Luna wagged her tail as Thor unfolded the paper, laying it flat on the ground between them. Neither could read human handwriting, but the paper smelled of lavender and old ink—a scent trail that would lead Sophie and Oliver straight to this treasure.

Thor sniffed at the paper, at Luna. "This is another important find, isn't it?" he said, his whiskers twitching. Luna barked softly, a gleam of intelligence in her eyes. Yes, this was significant, even if they couldn't understand why.

As Thor contemplated their next move, Luna nudged him gently with her nose. There was no time to ponder; the scent of an approaching human wafted into the cellar. Thor's eyes widened, and with a quick decision, he carefully slid the love letter underneath the mysterious bottle they had discovered earlier. Whoever the letter was from, and whoever it was meant for, it was a secret that needed to be shared.

Luna picked up the bottle in her mouth once again, making sure the letter was still tucked beneath it. As they made their way towards their secret exit, Thor paused and looked back. The cellar, with its barrels and old bottles, seemed to be waiting, as if holding its breath for the secrets to be unraveled.

The duo slipped out just as the sound of footsteps echoed closer and the door creaked open once more. Luna carefully placed the bottle and the hidden letter in a spot where their human counterparts couldn't miss them. Thor looked at Luna, his eyes gleaming in the dark.

"We did good today," Luna woofed, her tail wagging.

"Yes, we did," Thor meowed, his eyes meeting Luna's. "And something tells me this is just the beginning."

They retreated into the shadows, leaving behind the mysterious bottle and the hidden love letter—two pieces of a puzzle that would soon enthrall the whole town of Whistlewood. As they heard the surprised gasps of Sophie and Oliver discovering their finds, they knew their mission for the night was a success.

Yet as they nestled into their cozy beds, the sound of a distant car engine roared, and the scent of a new mystery wafted in the air. The adventure was far from over, and Luna's wagging tail and Thor's perked ears were proof that they were more than ready for whatever came next.

Sophie and Oliver walked into the cellar, each still immersed in their thoughts, holding candles that flickered and danced in the cool, dusky air. Sophie was contemplating the mysterious note she received, while Oliver was lost in thoughts about how to best support her amidst these challenges.

"Look, Oliver!" Sophie's eyes widened as she pointed at the mysterious bottle and the paper beside it, illuminated by the candlelight.

Startled out of his reverie, Oliver looked down. "You didn't leave that here earlier, did you?"

Sophie shook her head. "No, absolutely not. I've never seen that bottle or that paper before."

Oliver picked up the bottle, examining it closely. "This looks ancient. And look at this seal—it's from one of Whistlewood's earliest vineyards!"

Sophie's hands unfolded the paper. Her eyes scanned the faded writing, her mouth slowly opening in disbelief. "Oh my God, Oliver, this is a love letter—and it's addressed to the founder of this vineyard. It talks about a secret recipe for a unique wine blend and an unfulfilled love."

Oliver looked up, his eyes meeting Sophie's. "A secret wine blend? Do you think that's what's in this bottle?"

Sophie shrugged, her eyes filled with wonder. "There's only one way to find out."

, both of them heard a soft meow and a gentle woof from behind a wine barrel. Thor and Luna emerged, their eyes twinkling with what looked like a blend of pride and excitement.

"Wait a minute," Oliver said, glancing from the bottle and letter to Thor and Luna. "Did you two have something to do with this?"

If a cat could grin, Thor was doing it. And Luna's wagging tail spoke volumes.

Sophie chuckled. "It looks like they're more than just our pets; they're our guardian angels, leading us to clues and watching our backs."

Oliver put his arm around Sophie, pulling her close. "Well, they do say that pets and their owners become more alike over time. And we do love a good mystery."

As they looked down at Thor and Luna, Sophie's heart filled with a newfound courage. Perhaps the challenges they were facing weren't just obstacles but stepping stones leading them to a richer life full of undiscovered secrets and untold stories.

And as the two couples—human and pet—looked at each other in that dim, dusty cellar, each pair of eyes gleaming in the flickering candlelight, they all knew that this night was not the end but a thrilling beginning.

The curtain of one mystery might be falling, but the stage was already being set for the next. And whatever it was, they would face it together.

Brewing Suspicion

Luna, the Beagle with a keen nose for adventure, and Thor, a grey cat with an aura of feline wisdom, had always shared a bond thicker than water—or in this case, wine. Today, their intrigue led them to the vineyard's shadowy depths: the cellar.

The sun was setting, casting its golden glow over rows of grapevines, when Luna and Thor slipped through a small opening in the vineyard's cellar door. Dust particles danced in the slivers of sunlight that penetrated the dark room, illuminating rows of wooden barrels and racks of wine bottles.

Thor's whiskers twitched. "Something feels odd," he muttered, his green eyes narrowing.

Luna's ears perked up. "Odd how? Like the way a bone gets buried and forgotten?"

"Exactly," Thor responded. "This cellar keeps not only wine but also secrets."

The duo began their inspection. Thor leapt onto a barrel to gain a better view, while Luna sniffed the ground, her tail wagging with anticipation. Soon, her nose led her to a dusty corner where she discovered a set of old wine bottles, cobwebs veiling their labels.

Luna barked softly to get Thor's attention. The cat leapt down gracefully, landing beside her. He used a paw to swipe away the dust and cobwebs, revealing labels with mysterious symbols, not words.

"These aren't just any wine bottles; they're marked with the alchemy of winemaking—old family symbols, perhaps," Thor mused, his eyes widening.

Luna sniffed one of the bottles, her eyes meeting Thor's. "If Sophie knew about this, she could make something extraordinary!"

"Yes, but these aren't supposed to be here," Thor said, the weight of his words sinking in. "They've been deliberately hidden."

Luna and Thor exchanged a look of concern. They could sense a plot fermenting, a story far more complex than they'd anticipated. The bottles with the mysterious labels seemed to murmur an untold history, a narrative of love, betrayal, or perhaps, sabotage.

Realizing the gravity of their discovery, Luna's ears dropped low, and Thor's tail flicked anxiously. As they turned to leave, Luna's keen ears caught a sound—the creaking of the cellar door.

Someone was coming.

Thor and Luna were still in the cellar, debating whether to hide or make a quick exit, when Luna's keen ears picked up another sound, softer this time. It was a faint rustle, like paper being crumpled, coming from a crack in the old stone wall.

Curiosity piqued, Luna approached the wall, her nose twitching as she sniffed the air. She pawed gently at the crack, dislodging a small piece of folded parchment.

Thor jumped down from his perch atop a wine barrel, landing beside Luna. "What have you found now?" he asked, his eyes glinting with curiosity.

With her paw, Luna nudged the folded paper toward Thor. "Seems like something hidden, something forgotten."

Thor used his agile paws to unfold the paper, revealing faded ink handwriting that had stood the test of time. The words were elegant, the emotions raw. It was a love letter, heartfelt and desperate, speaking of a forbidden romance entangled in the vines of Whistlewood's past.

"Our love may never find the light of day, but like this wine, it shall age and mature in the secrecy of my heart," Thor read aloud, his voice tinged with emotion.

Luna sighed, her eyes softening. "Love that can't be shared—that's the saddest kind."

Both pets were struck by the profound sadness of the letter. Whoever wrote it had bottled up their feelings, much like the mysterious wines in the cellar.

Suddenly, Thor's eyes widened. "Look at this signature! It's the same symbol as the one on those wine bottles!"

Luna sniffed the letter, sniffed the mysterious bottle they had found earlier. The scent was identical.

"So, the wine and the letter are connected," Luna concluded. "But how? And why?"

Thor glanced at Luna, his eyes filled with gravity. "I think this vineyard has a history far more complex than any of us ever imagined. The story behind this letter could be the missing link."

Both pets realized they were onto something big, something that could affect not just the vineyard but the entire town of Whistlewood. Luna's tail stiffened, and Thor's whiskers twitched in anticipation.

Just as they were about to stash the letter somewhere safe, a noise echoed from the stairs leading to the cellar. Footsteps.

Sophie and Oliver, still carrying the remnants of a serious conversation about the strange note Sophie had received, descended into the vineyard cellar to sample some wine options for the Wine and Whimsy event. The atmosphere was laden with the fragrance of aged grapes and wood, and the temperature dropped several degrees as they reached the bottom of the staircase.

Sophie looked at Oliver, her eyes wide. "I hope we can find something really special here. The vineyard owner said they had some limited vintages tucked away."

Oliver nodded, but as he was about to reply, his gaze fell upon something on the floor—a tiny folded piece of parchment.

"What's this?" he said, picking it up and unfolding it carefully.

Sophie leaned over his shoulder to read. Her eyes widened as she saw the beautifully penned words of a heartfelt letter, filled with yearning and bittersweet love.

"It looks like someone's old love letter," she murmured, touched by the raw emotion in the lines.

Oliver nodded. "It's not just any love letter. Look, there's a symbol at the bottom. I've seen that symbol in some old winemaking books I was reading."

Sophie felt a shiver run down her spine. "Do you think it's related to the vineyard sabotage?"

Before Oliver could reply, they heard a faint scuffling sound from behind a row of wine barrels. Moving toward it, they found an old, dusty bottle with a mysterious label bearing the same symbol as in the love letter. Beside it were two paw prints—one feline, one canine.

Sophie grinned. "Looks like Thor and Luna have been doing some detective work of their own."

Oliver smiled back, his eyes meeting hers. "They've left us clues, Sophie. Clues that might lead us to understand what's going on."

Sophie felt a tingling sensation, like bubbles in champagne. She looked at Oliver, their eyes locking in a moment of mutual understanding and growing love.

"They've done their part," Sophie said softly. "Now it's time for us to do ours."

As they left the cellar, armed with the mysterious love letter and the clue-laden wine bottle, neither of them noticed the shadow that flitted away into the dark corners behind them. Their hearts were too full, their mission too clear.

But as they closed the door behind them, they both felt it: the weight of Whistlewood's untold secrets, waiting to be unraveled.

Petals and Proposals

Sophie stood in her flower shop, her fingers hesitating above an array of roses, lilies, and baby's breath. Normally, arranging flowers was her solace, her form of meditation, but today her thoughts kept drifting to the mysterious note she'd received. The words seemed to burn in her memory, raising questions and unsettling her usually cheerful spirit.

Oliver entered the shop, a smile on his face and a book in his hands. "Hey, I found this incredible vintage book on the art of wine and flower pairings. Thought it might interest you for the Wine and Whimsy event."

Sophie looked up, forcing a smile. "Oh, that sounds lovely, Oliver. Thank you."

But Oliver sensed her reticence immediately. "Something's bothering you, isn't it?"

Sophie sighed, setting down the flowers she was holding. "I can't shake off the feeling that note wasn't just some random act. What if someone is actually trying to sabotage the event? What if they're targeting me?"

Oliver stepped closer, taking her hand. "Sophie, we don't know who sent that note, but what I do know is that we can't let fear guide our actions. We should be cautious, yes, but we've also got a festival to prepare for."

Sophie nodded, but the worry lines remained on her forehead. "I know, you're right. It's just hard to focus when you feel like you're being watched or threatened."

Oliver squeezed her hand gently. "How about this? While we're preparing for the event, let's also keep an eye out for anything or anyone suspicious. We'll solve this mystery together."

As Sophie looked into Oliver's reassuring eyes, she felt a little of her anxiety ebb away. She knew he was right; they couldn't let anonymous threats derail their plans or their lives.

"Alright," she said, her voice stronger. "Let's prepare for the best Wine and Whimsy this town has ever seen—and let's also catch whoever is trying to ruin it."

Little did they know, as they reaffirmed their commitment to the event and each other, that the mysterious elements of Whistlewood were aligning in ways they couldn't yet comprehend.

The door chime of Sophie's flower shop jingled as Oliver made his exit, his heart feeling a curious blend of lightness and gravity. As he walked back to his bookstore, his hand slipped into the pocket of his tweed jacket, fingering the small velvet box that he'd been carrying for weeks now. He'd been waiting for the right moment, the perfect setting, to propose to Sophie, and as the Wine and Whimsy event approached, the idea took root that maybe, just maybe, the romantic atmosphere would offer just that.

Oliver settled into his leather armchair behind the counter of his bookstore, surrounded by the smell of old books—a scent that had always comforted him. But even the works of the great poets and novelists couldn't distract him now. He thought about the note Sophie had received, the threat looming over the upcoming festival, and a pang of worry mingled with his earlier enthusiasm. Could he really propose at a time like this?

Mrs. Harrington, Whistlewood's esteemed socialite, entered the shop, looking for a new mystery novel to indulge in. As Oliver recommended her a book, he found himself contemplating his own real-life mystery. Mrs. Harrington sensed his distraction and offered a piece of unsolicited but welcome advice: "My dear, in matters of the heart, there is no perfect time, only the right person."

As she left the store, her words echoed in Oliver's ears. Perhaps the uncertainties, the unresolved threats, were all the more reason to seize the moment and propose. Love, after all, was the greatest mystery of them all, wasn't it?

Slightly bolstered by this newfound resolve, Oliver opened the velvet box once again, staring at the ring. It was a vintage piece, with a blooming flower design, so reminiscent of Sophie herself. He imagined her eyes lighting up as he opened the box, the two of them surrounded by the rich scents of wine and flowers, amidst the melodies that would fill the Whistlewood air during the event.

Taking a deep breath, Oliver made up his mind. He would propose to Sophie at the Wine and Whimsy event, mysterious threats or not. And he'd make sure it would be a moment neither of them would ever forget.

The sun had set over Whistlewood, and the golden hour's glow turned into the soft luminance of the evening. The pre-event wine tasting was set in a charming courtyard, draped in twinkling fairy lights, providing a romantic touch to the cobblestone paths and blooming rose bushes that adorned the area. This evening, Oliver had chosen to put on a fine blazer while Sophie wore a flowing floral dress that made her seem as if she'd just stepped out of one of her own enchanting bouquets.

They were both determined to set aside the nagging worries about spoiled wine barrels and mysterious notes. Tonight, it was about them and their love for each other. "Isn't this wonderful?" Sophie mused as they entered the courtyard, her eyes lighting up at the sight of the elegantly dressed attendees and the delicate crystal wine glasses lined up on wooden tables.

"It is, absolutely," Oliver responded, his eyes meeting hers. "But not nearly as wonderful as you."

Sophie blushed. "Oh, stop it, you charmer."

They began their tasting journey at the first booth, where a sommelier from the local vineyard was offering samples of a fruity rosé. The wine danced delightfully on their palates, and for a moment, all seemed right with the world.

As they made their way through Cabernets and Pinots, Merlots and Chardonnays, the lingering tension started to melt away. Oliver's eyes frequently met Sophie's, and he was just about to convince himself that perhaps tonight would be the perfect moment to propose. That was when he saw her—Mrs. Harrington—engrossed in a hushed conversation with the vineyard owner. The vineyard owner had a concerned look, and Oliver felt the little bubble of happiness he'd been living in pop.

Sophie noticed his distraction. "What's wrong, Oliver? You look like you've just read a mystery's last page and didn't like the twist."

Oliver shook his head. "It's nothing. Let's enjoy the evening."

Just as they were about to toast with a sample of a particularly aromatic vintage, Sophie's phone buzzed. She glanced at the screen, and Oliver noticed a flicker of worry cross her face. "It's another note," she confessed. "An email this time."

Suddenly, the mood shifted. Oliver held Sophie's hand, trying to assure her without saying a word. They decided to take an early leave from the tasting, their hearts once again burdened with the concern that had briefly been lifted. As they walked back, Oliver pondered how they had transitioned from an evening that had promised to be a prelude to a celebration, to one that now felt like the introduction to a mystery neither wanted to solve but knew they had to.

But just as they were about to step out of the courtyard, Oliver stopped Sophie. "Even though tonight didn't end how we would've liked, I don't ever want to stop having these little moments with you—no matter the mysteries that lie ahead."

Sophie looked into his eyes and felt a tear form. "I wouldn't have it any other way, Oliver. We will get through this, like we always do."

As they walked hand-in-hand back home, both knew that the questions looming over the Wine and Whimsy event had cast a long shadow. But in that moment, the courage they drew from each other seemed enough light to guide their way.

Late Night Sneaks

The courtyard had finally emptied, the scent of wine and hors d'oeuvres still lingering in the air. Hiding behind a large, decorative barrel, Thor, the nimble grey cat, and Luna, the enthusiastic Beagle, kept their eyes on a particular worker from the vineyard. He had been acting peculiarly throughout the evening, especially when Mrs. Harrington and the vineyard owner were engrossed in their confidential conversation.

"Why are humans so complicated?" Luna wondered out loud, trying to make sense of the evening's events. "First the barrels, the notes, and now this."

Thor's eyes narrowed. "That's precisely why they need our help, Luna. There's mischief afoot, and we need to find out what it is."

After waiting for the worker to make a significant distance, Thor gave Luna a nod, and they both began to tail him, ducking behind shrubs, rosebushes, and stone walls. Luna's acute sense of smell proved valuable, and Thor's nimble agility allowed them to move without making a sound.

As they followed the worker, Luna couldn't help but think of Sophie. "Sophie looked so worried tonight," she mused. "She's been trying to make this special flower-wine, and these notes started coming."

Thor responded, "And Oliver hasn't been himself either. Something's unsettling him. We need to find out what's going on before it gets worse."

Finally, the worker led them to a secluded area near the edge of the vineyard, where numerous wine barrels were stored. Thor and Luna watched as he took a small vial from his pocket and poured its contents into one of the barrels, sealing it back hurriedly.

"Did you see that, Thor?" Luna whispered in disbelief. "He's ruining the wine!"

Thor's eyes gleamed in the darkness. "So, the rumors are true. Someone is sabotaging the vineyard, and now we know who."

Just as they were about to turn back and inform their human companions, Luna's ears picked up another sound—a faint, almost imperceptible rustle in the bushes behind them. Before they could react, another figure emerged from the shadows. It was the vineyard owner, and he had been watching the whole scene unfold from a distance.

"Mr. Miller!" Thor gasped. The vineyard owner was highly respected in Whistlewood, a generous man known for his love for the community. "What's he doing here? Does he know what his worker is up to?"

Luna's tail wagged nervously. "Or maybe he's part of this too? Oh, this is like one of those mystery novels Sophie reads!"

Suddenly, the vineyard owner pulled out his phone and snapped pictures of his worker tampering with the wine barrels. He looked furious, his face red and contorted with anger.

"He doesn't know," Thor concluded. "He's gathering evidence against his own worker. But why? Why not confront him right now?"

Luna pondered, "Maybe he's afraid there are others involved? This is becoming more twisted than I thought."

As the vineyard owner left the scene as quietly as he came, Thor looked at Luna and sighed, "It seems we've only scratched the surface of this mystery, Luna. This goes deeper than we thought, and it's not just about the wine."

Luna's ears perked up. "So what do we do now?"

Thor grinned, "Now, we dig deeper. Let's go tell Sophie and Oliver what we've found. They need to know, and we have a festival to save."

As they made their way back, a feeling of urgency overcame them. The mystery was unraveling, but the answers they sought seemed as elusive as ever. One thing was clear, though; they were in this together, and come what may, they would get to the bottom of it.

After informing Sophie and Oliver of the disturbing developments through an elaborate dance of paws and meows, which only their keen owners could understand, Thor and Luna knew they had to act fast. There was evidence to gather, and a festival's reputation—as well as the good name of Whistlewood's finest vineyard—to uphold. The twosome set their eyes on the worker's residence, an old cottage at the end of the vineyard.

The moon was high in the sky, casting eerie shadows on the ground as Luna and Thor approached the cottage. "Be on your guard, Luna," Thor whispered. "We don't know what we're walking into."

Luna nodded, sniffing the air cautiously. "Something smells.. . chemical."

They waited until they were sure the coast was clear. With a quiet agility that belied her size, Luna leapt onto a ledge below a slightly open window and nudged it further open with her nose. Thor, lithe and agile, slipped in first, landing softly on a worn carpet. Luna followed suit.

Inside, the house was dark, save for the moonlight streaming through the window. Thor's eyes adjusted quickly, scanning the room. "This way," he signaled with his tail, leading Luna to a closed door beneath the stairs.

The door was ajar, revealing a room filled with shelves of glass jars, vials, and what looked like small chemistry equipment. Luna's eyes widened. "This looks like a mad scientist's lab," she said, sniffing at the various substances. "These chemicals... they're what's being used to spoil the wine!"

Thor leapt onto a table and examined the labels on some of the jars. "Cyanides, sulfites, even acetone. This is a dangerous stash, Luna. This goes beyond simple sabotage; it's criminal."

While Luna looked around, her eyes caught a notebook lying beside a set of scales. With a sense of urgency, she nudged it open. It was filled with handwritten notes, measurements, and, disturbingly, a list of names—many of which were key members of Whistlewood.

"Thor, look at this," Luna said. "There are names here. Mrs. Harrington, the vineyard owner Mr. Miller, even Sophie is mentioned!"

Thor glanced through the notebook quickly. "This is a revenge plot, Luna, a dangerous and calculated one. We need to get this evidence to Sophie and Oliver immediately."

As they were about to leave, Luna's sensitive ears picked up the sound of footsteps approaching the cottage. "Someone's coming!" she whispered, her heart pounding.

In a split second, the duo bolted back the way they had come, narrowly making it out the window as the front door creaked open. Hidden behind the thick bushes, they watched the worker enter his cottage. Their hearts sank when they saw him holding another vial in his hands.

"This isn't over," Thor said, his eyes narrowing. "It's far from over."

Luna looked at her feline companion. "We have enough to expose him, but we have to act fast, Thor. Who knows what he's planning for the festival?"

Thor's whiskers twitched thoughtfully. "You're right, Luna. Timing is of the essence now. We've unraveled a secret, but solving this mystery may be more dangerous than we thought."

Both pets looked at each other, knowing the gravity of the situation. They had dug deep into the corrupt underbelly of what seemed like a whimsical festival, and now there was no turning back. The comfort of their loving homes seemed like a distant memory; they were investigators, protectors of Whistlewood, and they would see this through to the end.

Thor and Luna burst out of their hiding spot, their paws pounding the earth as they raced back towards home. Their hearts were pumping wildly, each beat echoing the gravity of what they had discovered.

"Go, go, go!" Thor's meow was more of a growl as he urged Luna on. The Beagle's strong legs carried her swiftly, her nose pointed straight ahead like an arrow. Both animals knew they couldn't afford to be caught; the evidence they had uncovered was too critical.

As they reached the midpoint of the vineyard, Luna heard a rustling sound behind them. "Thor, he's following us!"

Sure enough, when Thor risked a glance back, he saw the figure of the worker emerging from the cottage. He was holding a flashlight, its beam darting around in the dark like a predatory eye. "Faster, Luna!" he hissed.

The pets pushed their muscles to the limit, adrenaline fuelling their desperate sprint. Yet even as they neared the edge of the vineyard, a shout echoed behind them, and the beam of the flashlight swept perilously close to their tails.

"Almost there, Thor!" Luna barked, but her words were cut off when a sharp object whizzed past them, embedding itself in a nearby tree.

"Throwing knives? This guy is serious!" Thor's eyes widened as the urgency of the situation redoubled. They had to reach Sophie and Oliver. They had to.

Finally, after what felt like an eternity, they crossed the threshold from the vineyard to the main road leading to their homes. But just as they thought they had made it, the worker's voice rang out, chillingly close. "You won't escape!"

Luna felt her heart freeze for a split second, but Thor leapt at her, pushing her to the side just as another object sliced through the air where she had just been. Rolling back onto her paws, she gave Thor a nod of thanks. "Last stretch, buddy."

Drawing on their last reserves of strength, they sprinted up the road, their eyes fixated on the comforting lights of Whistlewood's charming houses. As they reached Sophie's flower shop, they darted around the back, squeezing through a small opening in the fence that led to the garden.

They had made it, but their tiny chests heaved with exertion, their paws aching.

"Quick, we need to alert them," Thor said, his whiskers twitching as he started to pace around, thinking of ways to communicate the urgency of what they had found.

Luna's ears perked up as she heard footsteps inside the house. A moment later, the back door opened, and out stepped Sophie and Oliver, deep in conversation.

The couple froze when they saw the state their pets were in—panting, disheveled, clearly agitated. "What on earth happened to you two?" Sophie exclaimed, kneeling down to examine Luna.

"Something's wrong," Oliver said, picking up Thor and meeting his eyes. In that moment, the bond between pet and owner conveyed more than any words could.

The couple looked at each other, their faces turning grave. "I think they found something, something critical," Sophie said softly.

" we need to act, now," Oliver replied, his grip tightening around Thor. "The festival is at stake, but it feels like there's more to it than that."

As Sophie held Luna and Oliver held Thor, both pets knew their message had been received. They had dodged a knife—both literally and metaphorically—and while they had avoided being caught tonight, they were diving deeper into a mystery that was proving to be as dangerous as it was convoluted.

It was a perilous path they were on, but at least they weren't walking it alone.

The Vintage Vendetta

Sophie turned the key in the lock and pushed open the door, her arms laden with flowers for tomorrow's arrangements. The moment she stepped inside, however, she knew something was off. The air felt different—charged, somehow.

"Oliver, are you home?" she called out, setting down the flowers on the kitchen table. When she received no answer, a wave of dread washed over her.

Her eyes darted around the room, landing on a shattered picture frame lying on the floor. It was a photo of her and Oliver at last year's Wine and Whimsy event—a picture that had always sat on the mantle. Her heart sank.

, the front door swung open, and Oliver stepped in, his face lighting up when he saw her. "Sophie, I've got great news! The biographies I ordered for the festival finally—"

His voice trailed off when he saw her pale face and the broken frame on the ground. "What happened here?"

Sophie could only shake her head, tears forming in her eyes. Oliver quickly took in the disarray—the open drawers, the rifled-through bookshelves, and a sense of violation filled him.

"Someone's been here, Ollie," Sophie whispered. "Someone broke into our home."

Oliver clenched his fists, his initial excitement now replaced by a protective fury. "I'll call the police. We need to know what's been taken, what they were after."

Sophie nodded, but her eyes were on Luna and Thor, who had just entered the room, their faces as anxious as she felt. It was as if they understood that their sanctuary had been invaded, that the walls meant to keep them safe had been breached.

As Oliver reported the break-in, Sophie sat on the couch, Luna climbing up beside her, while Thor leapt onto the backrest, his eyes narrowed and tail flicking side to side. Even without understanding the complexity of human emotions, the pets sensed the disquiet that had settled over their owners, and by extension, over them.

By the time Oliver ended the call, Sophie was holding one of Thor's paws, and Luna had laid her head on Sophie's lap. Their physical closeness was some comfort, but it did little to dispel the invisible cloud that now hung over them.

"We'll get through this, Soph," Oliver said, sitting next to her and pulling her into a hug. "We have each other, and we have Luna and Thor. We're not alone in this."

Sophie nodded against his chest, drawing a shaky breath. "I know we will, but what scares me is how this is connected to everything else—the festival, the vineyard, and now this."

Oliver kissed the top of her head. "We'll figure it out, one step at a time."

But as they held each other, trying to reclaim some sense of normalcy, neither could shake the feeling that this break-in was more than just an isolated event. It was a message, a foreboding omen that things in Whistlewood were about to take a darker turn. And the worst part was, they had no idea how dark things could get.

Sophie finally pulled away from Oliver's embrace, wiping her eyes with the back of her hand. "We should start cleaning up," she said, forcing herself to focus on the task at hand.

Oliver nodded, gathering the broken picture frame from the floor and setting it on the table. "I'll get a broom. We can sort through this mess—"

His voice trailed off as his eyes landed on something odd by the bookshelf. A small, transparent vial lay there, partially hidden by the fringe of the area rug.

"What's this?" He picked it up cautiously, eyeing the dark liquid inside.

Sophie joined him, Luna and Thor trailing behind. The sight of the vial brought a flash of recognition in Sophie's eyes. "This... this looks exactly like the chemical sample that ruined the wine at the vineyard. But how did it get here?"

Oliver turned the vial over in his hand. "Could it have fallen out of the thief's pocket? That seems unlikely—"

Thor jumped onto the bookshelf, his paw nudging another smaller vial hidden behind some books.

"What the—? Another one?" Oliver retrieved the second vial. Unlike the first, this one was empty but smelled strongly of chemicals.

Luna barked softly, her eyes meeting Sophie's as if to say, "Pay attention to us."

Sophie knelt down to pat Luna and noticed something around her collar—a tiny scrap of paper, folded and wedged into the fabric. She carefully took it out and unfolded it. It was a hastily written note: "Vineyard, midnight."

"This looks like a message," Sophie said, showing it to Oliver. "And I think Luna and Thor left it for us. But what does it mean?"

Oliver looked from the note to the vials and back to Sophie, his brow furrowed in deep thought. "If I had to guess, I'd say our pets have been doing some detective work of their own. And whatever they found, it led them back here."

A sudden realization washed over Sophie, bringing with it both awe and fear. "Oliver, do you think Luna and Thor know who's behind the sabotage?"

"I wouldn't be surprised," Oliver answered, equally awestruck by the intelligence of their pets. "And if that's true, we're more involved in this mystery than we thought."

"Involved, or targeted?" Sophie murmured, gripping the vial in her hand.

Oliver clenched his jaw, his eyes filled with steely resolve. "Either way, we need to get to the bottom of this. For us, for Whistlewood, and especially for Luna and Thor. They're trying to tell us something, and we need to listen."

As they stood there, holding the chemical vials and the cryptic note, Luna and Thor exchanged glances. If they could understand the gravity of the situation, they would have felt the same sense of urgency that Sophie and Oliver now felt.

This was no longer just about a ruined festival or spoiled wine. This was personal. And the four of them—two humans and their fiercely loyal pets—were now united in a common, dangerous quest for the truth.

Oliver set the vials and the cryptic note on the coffee table, went over to his laptop. With deft keystrokes, he began searching through various chemical databases.

"Are you going to cross-reference the chemical with the ones used in winemaking?" Sophie asked, her eyes still fixed on the mysterious vials.

"Exactly. If it matches the chemicals found in the spoiled wine, this isn't just mere coincidence." Oliver's eyes scanned the screen rapidly as he navigated through chemical formulas and data sheets.

After a tense ten minutes, his eyes widened. "I've got it," he declared, pointing at a specific chemical formula on the screen. "This matches the chemical found in the sabotaged barrels."

Sophie felt her heart race as she joined Oliver to look at the screen. "So it's the same chemical, then? We're definitely being targeted."

"It looks that way," Oliver confirmed, shutting his laptop. "And if Luna and Thor have left us these clues, they might know who's behind it."

Sophie's eyes fell on Luna and Thor, who sat patiently by the door, as if waiting for their next mission. "We have to do something, Oliver. If this person is willing to break into our home, who knows what they might do next?"

"You're right," Oliver said, his voice filled with determination. "We can't sit idly by anymore. We have to find out who's behind this and why they're doing it, not just for us, but for the entire community. The Wine and Whimsy festival is important to Whistlewood, and we can't let it be ruined."

Sophie picked up the note Luna had carried. "Vineyard, midnight. That's tonight. Do you think we should go?"

"Absolutely," Oliver said. "It's a risk, but it's one we have to take. Whoever this is, they're threatening our town, our friends, and our life together. We can't let them win."

They locked eyes, and in that moment, a new resolve settled over them. They were united in purpose, drawn together not just by love but by a burning need to protect their home and each other.

Sophie clenched her fist around the note. " let's do it. For Whistlewood, for the festival, and for ourselves."

As they started to prepare for their midnight foray, they had no idea what awaited them. But one thing was clear: they were in this together, come what may, ready to face the truth that was bubbling beneath the surface of their idyllic town.

And so, under the watchful eyes of Luna and Thor, Sophie and Oliver prepared to dive headfirst into a mystery that was more tangled and dangerous than any vineyard grapevine.

Unearthed Secrets

Sophie was in the living room, sifting through some old books Oliver had brought from the bookstore, hoping they might contain information on local vineyards. To her surprise, a folded newspaper clipping fell out of one of the books.

"Oliver, come look at this," she called out, smoothing the aged paper on the coffee table.

Curious, Oliver joined her and peered at the headline: "Decades-Old Feud Between Vineyard Families Threatens to Sour Grapes." Below, an old black and white photo showed two patriarchs of Whistlewood's renowned vineyard families, scowling at each other.

"Wow, talk about a blast from the past," Oliver said. "I vaguely remember hearing about this feud when I was a kid, but I had no idea it was this serious."

Sophie scanned the article quickly. "According to this, the feud was about land rights and unique grape strains. Both families accused each other of sabotage, much like what we're facing now."

Oliver sat down, looking intrigued. "Do you think this feud might be connected to our situation? The spoiled wine, the sabotage?"

Sophie considered it. "It's a possibility. Old grudges die hard, especially in small towns. Maybe someone's trying to settle a score."

"Or revive the feud for a new generation," Oliver added, his eyes narrowing. "Either way, we have to dig deeper. This might be the key to understanding why the vineyard was targeted."

Sophie nodded, clutching the newspaper clipping. "I agree. We need to go back in time to figure out what's happening in the present. If history is repeating itself, we should know why."

As they discussed their next steps, Luna and Thor watched them intently, their eyes gleaming as if they sensed the importance of the discovery. With each unraveling clue, Sophie and Oliver grew more certain that solving this mystery was not just about the festival or the vineyard; it was about uprooting the weeds of discord that threatened to engulf their community.

Luna's nose was twitching uncontrollably as she and Thor prowled through the shadowy corners of the vineyard's dimly lit cellar. She caught whiffs of dust, mold, and aged wine, but also something else—an aroma that couldn't quite be placed, but was undeniably intriguing.

"Do you smell that, Thor?" Luna whispered, her eyes scanning the labyrinth of wooden wine racks and ancient barrels.

Thor's whiskers twitched as he sniffed the air. "Yes. Something's off. I suggest we follow it."

With Luna in the lead, they made their way deeper into the cellar, skirting past cobwebs and half-broken crates until they reached a dead end. Or at least, it seemed like a dead end. Luna's nose was still twitching.

She began sniffing the wall at the far end of the cellar, pawed at it, her claws clicking against what sounded like hollow wood. "There's something behind here. I can feel it."

Thor jumped up to inspect a seemingly out-of-place lever hidden among some old pipes near the ceiling. "Luna, give me a boost. I think I've found something."

With a running start, Luna lunged at the wall, providing just enough of a step for Thor to leap and pull down the lever with his paw. The wall before them creaked and slowly swung open, revealing a hidden room.

They stepped inside, their eyes widening at the sight before them. Stacks of old documents, mysterious bottles with handwritten labels, and what looked like detailed blueprints of the vineyard filled the hidden chamber. But what caught their attention most was a corkboard at the far end of the room. Pinned to it were recent photographs of Sophie and Oliver, along with maps and a timeline.

"This is serious, Thor," Luna said, her eyes locking with his. "Someone's been planning something sinister for a long time, and it involves Sophie and Oliver."

"We need to alert them," Thor said, his eyes sharp and determined. "But first, let's grab something that can serve as evidence."

Luna carefully picked up a small vial filled with a mysterious substance—perhaps another type of chemical—while Thor pawed a few of the documents into a neat pile. They made sure to leave everything else as they found it, not wanting to alert whoever was behind this that their secret room had been discovered.

As they made their way back through the now-less-mysterious cellar, both pets felt a chill run down their spines. Luna glanced at Thor, her eyes reflecting her growing unease. "Let's get this evidence to Sophie and Oliver. They need to know what's happening, and fast."

Sophie and Oliver sat in the dimly lit courtyard of their favorite little café. A string of fairy lights hung above their heads, casting a soft glow over the table. Plates of finished dessert and near-empty glasses of wine adorned the tabletop. The atmosphere was intimate, the night quiet but for the distant sound of a violin serenading the sleepy streets of Whistlewood.

Sophie looked lost in thought, her gaze drifting over the intricate floral patterns that graced the café's wrought-iron fence. She was still shaken from the odd events surrounding the vineyard and the mounting threats. She sighed deeply, causing Oliver to reach across the table and take her hand.

"Hey," he said softly, his eyes searching hers. "You seem far away."

"I'm just worried," Sophie admitted. "About the vineyard, the festival, and well, us."

Oliver's heart sank a little, but he understood her anxiety. The strange occurrences had put them both on edge. Yet in that moment, he realized that there was never going to be a perfect time for life-altering decisions. Sometimes, one had to make their own perfect moments.

"Sophie," he began, pushing back his chair and getting down on one knee. The entire café seemed to pause, the background noises fading away until all that remained was the electric tension of the moment. "I know times are uncertain and the world is full of chaos, but one thing has always been clear to me. I love you, and I want to face all of life's mysteries with you."

Sophie's eyes filled with tears, her hand flying up to her mouth in surprise. For a moment, she was speechless, caught in a whirlwind of emotion and surprise.

Oliver reached into his pocket and produced a small, velvet box. As he opened it to reveal a delicate ring, he looked up into Sophie's eyes. "Will you marry me?"

Time stood still as Sophie looked at Oliver, her heart pounding in her chest. Then, as if breaking free from a trance, she finally spoke. "Yes, Oliver. A thousand times yes."

Cheers erupted from the surrounding tables, and even the violinist in the corner began playing a lively tune. Oliver slipped the ring onto Sophie's finger before standing up to pull her into a passionate embrace. The kiss they shared was unlike any other; it was a promise, a thank you, and a proclamation all in one.

As they broke apart, both of their faces glowing with love and happiness, they knew that regardless of the trials that awaited them, they would face them together. And that was all that truly mattered.

A Starlit
Confrontation

With a newfound determination and a knot of urgency in his stomach, Oliver walked into the Whistlewood Police Station. The air was thick with the aroma of stale coffee and printer ink. The officers behind their desks looked up briefly, recognizing him as a town regular but clearly not expecting him to be their next case.

"Good morning, Officer Johnson. I have something important to discuss. May I speak to the chief?" Oliver's voice was steady, despite the rapid beating of his heart.

Officer Johnson, a stout man with graying hair and an unyielding posture, sighed and gestured toward Chief Miller's office at the back. "Go on, he's in."

Taking a deep breath to calm his racing heart, Oliver approached the half-open door and knocked gently.

"Come in," a gruff voice called out.

Chief Miller looked up from a pile of paperwork that seemed to mirror the towering stacks that surrounded his cluttered desk. He was a tall, imposing man, yet his eyes held an unmistakable warmth.

"Oliver, to what do I owe the pleasure? Here to donate some books to the station?" Chief Miller asked, forcing a light-hearted tone but seeing the serious expression on Oliver's face.

"No, Chief, this is something much more pressing," Oliver began, taking the seat across the desk and laying down a manila folder. "I've found substantial evidence that points to the sabotage of the upcoming Wine and Whimsy event."

Chief Miller's eyebrows shot up, intrigued but visibly skeptical. "Sabotage, you say?"

Opening the folder, Oliver carefully laid out the information. He explained the chemical samples that Thor and Luna had found and detailed the old newspaper clippings revealing an ancient feud between vineyard families in Whistlewood. He also told the chief about the spoiled barrels of wine and the break-in at Sophie's shop.

Chief Miller listened intently, the skepticism slowly retreating from his eyes. When Oliver finally finished, a heavy silence filled the room before the chief finally spoke. "Oliver, this is a serious accusation. You're aware that if this is some kind of prank, there are legal consequences?"

"I assure you, Chief, this is as serious as it gets. Our livelihoods, our traditions, and even our personal safety might be at risk," Oliver's voice was filled with earnest concern, leaving no room for doubt.

For a long moment, the chief locked eyes with Oliver. Then, finally, he nodded. "Alright. I'll take it from here. You've done good, Oliver. I'll have my officers look into this immediately."

As Oliver left the police station, he couldn't help but feel a mixture of relief and trepidation. They had crossed a significant hurdle, yes, but the road ahead was fraught with uncertainty. Would they catch the culprit in time to save the Wine and Whimsy event, let alone Sophie's floral business? And how would this affect his future with Sophie, especially now that they were engaged?

While his mind was awash with questions, Oliver felt a certain pride in knowing that at least now the powers that be were on their side. With the police involved, they were one step closer to unraveling the dangerous mystery that loomed over Whistlewood.

As Oliver stepped into the crisp autumn air, he thought of Sophie, of Thor and Luna, and of the close-knit community they had built together. He realized that no matter how dire things seemed, they had each other—and that gave him all the courage he needed to face whatever came next.

The day was unusually hectic at Sophie's floral shop, "Blossom & Vine." Customers flowed in and out, asking about her latest floral arrangements and the recently talked-about flower-infused wines. News had spread like wildfire that Sophie's unique wine contributions could be the last hope for the festival. As she tied a ribbon around a bouquet of daffodils, her thoughts were consumed by the festival, now just days away.

Oliver walked into the shop, carrying a bag of her favorite lavender macarons. Seeing his face instantly lifted Sophie's spirits.

"I thought you could use a pick-me-up," Oliver said with a warm smile, placing the bag on the counter.

"You read my mind," Sophie beamed, stealing a quick kiss before sharing the latest developments. "Guess what? The town council just confirmed they'd love to feature my floral wines at the festival!"

"That's fantastic, Soph! You're saving the day!" Oliver's eyes sparkled with pride.

Sophie bit her lip, a shadow of concern passing over her. "I hope so. The pressure's on, and my wine experiments are no longer just whimsical side projects. They're crucial now."

Understanding her anxiety, Oliver reassured her. "Soph, you're incredibly talented, and people love what you create. I have no doubt your wines will be the talk of the festival."

Sophie sighed, her shoulders dropping as if a weight had been lifted. "Thank you, Oliver. Your faith in me means the world."

, a notification popped up on Sophie's phone. It was an email from the vineyard owner, stating that the investigation was making headway and thanking her for her invaluable wine contributions that would help save the festival's reputation.

"Look at this, Oliver," she said, showing him the email.

He read it and grinned. "See? Even the vineyard owner agrees with me."

As they shared a moment of triumph, Sophie couldn't shake off a sense of impending drama. It was as if the air in Whistlewood had thickened, waiting for a storm to break. The weight of the festival's success now partially rested on her shoulders, and the last thing she wanted was to let anyone down.

Then, her phone buzzed again, startling her. It was a text message from an unknown number.

"Be careful, the spotlight can burn you as easily as it can warm you."

Sophie felt her blood run cold. This veiled threat didn't feel like a random message but rather a calculated attempt to scare her. She showed it to Oliver, who clenched his fists, anger flashing in his eyes.

"We can't let this intimidate us. We'll tell Chief Miller right away," Oliver declared.

Sophie nodded, grateful that the police were now taking their concerns seriously. Little did they know that this festival, meant to be a simple celebration of their community, would become the epicenter of a battle they never asked for, but were now fully committed to winning.

And as she looked at Oliver, a thought crossed her mind: This festival was not just a celebration of wine and whimsy. It was now a test, a defining moment for their relationship and the entire Whistlewood community.

The moon hung low in the night sky, casting long shadows across the cobblestone streets of Whistlewood. The town seemed to hold its breath, as if in anticipation of something extraordinary. Luna, the astute beagle with a nose for trouble, and Thor, the nimble grey cat with eyes like saucers, shared an instinctual understanding that tonight would be a turning point in their covert investigation.

"Stay close, Luna," Thor whispered as he led the way, his tail flicking cautiously.

"Right behind you, furball," Luna responded, her eyes never leaving the path before them.

They had spotted the mysterious stranger leaving the vineyard earlier that evening during the wine tasting event. Now they were tailing him discreetly, their four-legged gaits both silent and swift.

The stranger turned into an alley, eventually stopping in front of a nondescript wooden door, barely visible in the dim light. He looked around furtively before entering, the door creaking shut behind him.

"This must be it," Luna said, her nose twitching as if to confirm her suspicion.

"Let's go in," Thor suggested, and they approached the door cautiously.

It wasn't locked. Thor nudged it open with his paw, and the two of them slipped inside. The room was dark, save for a single flickering light bulb that barely illuminated the surroundings. Crates were stacked against the walls, and an old desk stood in the middle of the room. A corkboard hung on the wall, filled with what appeared to be timelines and plans.

"Our human friends need to see this," Luna remarked, scanning the room with her eyes and nose.

"I agree, but how do we get them here without drawing attention?" Thor wondered.

, they heard footsteps approaching the door. Their eyes met, a mutual understanding flashing between them: they had to leave, and fast. But not before Luna, using her mouth, snatched a small piece of paper that had fallen on the floor—a note or perhaps a clue of some kind.

They dashed out the door just as it opened, their hearts pounding in their chests. The stranger walked in, seemingly unaware of their presence. However, as he entered, he paused, as if sensing something amiss.

Luna and Thor retreated to a hidden corner, their breaths shallow and quick. They had found something critical, but the danger had never felt more real.

"Now what?" Luna asked, still clutching the piece of paper in her mouth.

"We alert Sophie and Oliver, but we have to be smarter this time. This is bigger than we thought," Thor replied, his whiskers twitching anxiously.

As they made their way back through the moonlit streets of Whistlewood, Luna couldn't help but think about the upcoming festival. For a celebration that was supposed to bring joy and unity, it had unearthed secrets, tensions, and now dangers that no one had anticipated.

"Are we in over our heads?" she asked, looking up at Thor.

"In over our whiskers, maybe. But that's never stopped us before," he said, a newfound determination in his eyes.

Little did they know that their nighttime escapade had changed the course of their investigation. And with the Wine and Whimsy festival just around the corner, time was running out.

Corked Resolutions

It was the evening before the Wine and Whimsy event, and the vine-yard was abuzz with last-minute preparations. Sophie, her vibrant blue eyes shimmering in the waning sunlight, felt a wave of exhilaration as she gazed upon the crates of flower-infused wines she had crafted. Her heart swelled with pride and a hint of trepidation. Oliver, absorbed in a manuscript on ancient winemaking techniques, looked up and caught her eye. He smiled, instantly calming her jitters.

However, this sense of serenity was short-lived. As Oliver flipped through the pages, something caught his eye. "Do you hear that?" he asked, pausing to listen. A commotion was coming from the far corner of the vineyard, near the old oak tree that marked the boundary between the vines and the forest.

"Sounds like shouting," Sophie responded, concerned. "Let's go see what's going on."

They walked hurriedly toward the source of the noise, their foot-steps crunching on the gravel path. As they approached, they noticed a group of vineyard workers gathered in a tight circle. They seemed agitated, gesturing wildly at something—or someone—in their midst.

"What's happening here?" Sophie asked, her voice tinged with con-cern as they broke through the crowd.

"Caught these two sneaking around," one worker said, pointing at two individuals who looked as out of place as a sunflower in a sea of roses.

The suspects, a man and a woman dressed in nondescript clothing, looked uncomfortable but not overly alarmed.

"We were just curious about the festival," the man stammered, avoiding eye contact. "Wanted to see if we could help."

"By sneaking around? That's a strange way to offer help," Oliver said, skeptical of the man's weak explanation.

, Luna and Thor emerged from behind a barrel, their eyes locking onto the suspects. Both pets seemed unusually alert, their senses fully engaged.

The atmosphere grew palpable, thick with suspicion and mounting questions. Oliver felt a surge of protectiveness. He thought of the spoiled barrels of wine, the mysterious note, and Sophie's jeopardized experiments. Could these strangers be involved? Were they the unknown variables in an equation that was becoming increasingly complex and perilous?

Sophie sensed Oliver's growing tension and took his hand. Her touch was a gentle reminder of the life they were building together, amidst the chaos that had recently enveloped them. But it also strengthened his resolve.

"We need to inform the police," Oliver said firmly, "and keep a close eye on things until this is all sorted out. Something isn't right here."

Sophie nodded, and as they retreated from the crowd, she couldn't shake off a feeling of dread. The festival that was supposed to celebrate love and community was becoming a backdrop for darker, more troubling narratives.

, Thor brushed against Sophie's leg, as if comforting her. She looked down and noticed a folded piece of paper clutched in Luna's mouth. Intrigued, she took it from her and opened it up. What she saw made her heart skip a beat. It was a detailed map of the vineyard, with several locations circled in red.

"What on earth is this?" Oliver exclaimed as he looked at the paper, his eyes widening in disbelief.

The moon had risen in the Whistlewood sky, casting a silvery glow over the vineyard. Oliver, holding the mysterious map tightly in his hand, paced back and forth, trying to make sense of it all.

"We have to do something about this, and fast," Sophie whispered, her eyes meeting Oliver's. "Whatever they're planning, it's happening tonight. Look at the date marked on the map."

"Yes, but how do we catch them without jeopardizing ourselves or the festival?" Oliver wondered aloud.

, Thor started to circle around them, his tail flicking with an air of urgency. Luna, her eyes sharp and intelligent, nudged a piece of rope toward Sophie and Oliver.

"Are you thinking what I'm thinking?" Oliver grinned, looking at the animals.

"I believe so," Sophie chuckled. "Thor and Luna want to set a trap."

They quickly divided their responsibilities. Sophie would use her knowledge of herbs to create a scent trail leading to a location where they could safely corner the suspects. Oliver, using his tactical understanding gleaned from countless mystery novels, would position himself in a vantage point to observe their movements. Thor and Luna, the brave and adorable bait, would lure the suspects into the trap.

Each taking one end of the rope, Sophie and Oliver rigged a simple but effective snare, hidden among the grapevines near the circled area on the map. As a finishing touch, Sophie sprayed a mist of lavender and sage—scents too enticing to resist.

Once everything was set, they retreated to their hiding spots. Thor and Luna sat conspicuously near the trap, looking as nonchalant as a cat and dog possibly could.

Minutes turned into an eternity as they waited, each lost in their thoughts. Oliver questioned the morality of their actions. Was it right to take matters into their own hands? Yet, looking at Sophie—strong, intelligent, vibrant—he realized they had no choice but to protect what they loved.

Sophie sensed the tension thickening the air. Just when she started to doubt, a rustling sound caught her ear, growing louder and more focused. She held her breath.

Two figures emerged from the shadows, their faces masked. They looked around cautiously and started to follow the scent trail Sophie had laid. Nearing the trap, they paused to look at Thor and Luna.

"Isn't that cute, a cat and a dog," one of them said, bending down to pet them.

That was the cue. Sophie and Oliver tightened the rope, effectively trapping the duo.

The tension in the vineyard was almost palpable as Sophie kept her eyes trained on the suspect reaching for his pocket. Her hand instinctively grabbed Oliver's, fingers entwined in a tangle of fear and resolve.

Before she could utter a word of caution, Thor sprang forward with an agile leap, knocking the object from the man's hand. It clattered on the ground—a pocket knife. Luna barked, a loud, assertive sound that seemed to declare victory.

, the flashing red and blue lights pierced through the vineyard's misty darkness, and the wailing siren came to a halt. The police had arrived, right on cue.

"Whistlewood Police! Nobody move!" shouted Officer Williams, as he and his team emerged from the squad car, handcuffs ready.

Sophie and Oliver stepped aside as the officers swiftly handcuffed the suspects and read them their rights. Another officer picked up the pocket knife as evidence.

"You two okay?" Officer Williams asked, concerned eyes surveying Sophie and Oliver.

"We're fine, thanks to Thor and Luna," Sophie replied, gesturing to their brave pets who were now sniffing around as if nothing extraordinary had happened.

"Yeah," Oliver chimed in. "You'll want to take a look at this," he said, handing over the mysterious map they had used to set the trap.

Officer Williams studied the map, looked back at the couple. "Well, it seems like Whistlewood owes you two—and your furry friends—a debt of gratitude. We've been after these guys for weeks."

As the suspects were led away, one of them sneered, "This isn't over. You don't know what you've gotten into."

Sophie felt a chill but squeezed Oliver's hand for reassurance. Whatever lay ahead, they would face it together.

The Last Toast

Sophie and Oliver stood in the quaint attic of Oliver's bookstore, surrounded by antique furniture, cobwebbed windows, and old cartons filled with remnants of the past. At the center of their focus was a glass-encased table, upon which lay an intricately designed amulet: a grape cluster wrought in gold with tiny gemstones for the fruit. It shimmered in the sparse light coming through the attic window.

"Can you believe it, Oliver? This heirloom is connected to the vineyard feud!" Sophie's voice was tinged with a blend of excitement and disbelief.

Oliver, carefully handling a sheaf of yellowed newspapers, looked up and met her gaze. "These clippings mention a family heirloom, but it's bizarre that we found it here. Do you think this could be the very one that instigated the feud between the two vineyard families?"

Sophie picked up the amulet cautiously, feeling its weight and absorbing its history. "There's a sense of deep-rooted bitterness and untold stories in this piece of jewelry. I think it's time we delved further into this feud and find out how this heirloom is related."

Her eyes turned to a corner of the attic where her pets, Thor and Luna, were amusing themselves by batting at a stray ball of yarn. "And I'm sure our furry detectives will want to dig into this too," she chuckled.

Just as she said this, Luna, the inquisitive Beagle, trotted over and sniffed at the amulet. Thor followed, his eyes narrowing as though analyzing the piece's historical value.

Sophie looked at Oliver, who was engrossed in another newspaper clipping. "What does it say?"

Clearing his throat, Oliver began, "According to this article from 1962, a missing heirloom caused a significant rift between the two prominent vineyard families of Whistlewood—The Gardiners and the McAllisters. It says here that the heirloom was considered a good luck charm that made the vineyards prosperous. Both families blamed each other for its disappearance."

Sophie, placing the amulet back on the table, sighed. "So much lost over a piece of metal and stone. But how did it end up here in your bookstore, Oliver?"

Before Oliver could answer, Thor jumped onto the table, and with his paw, he pushed aside a pile of papers to reveal an old photograph. It was a black-and-white image of a man standing beside grapevines, the same amulet hanging prominently around his neck.

"That's my grandfather!" Oliver exclaimed, recognition washing over his face. "I remember seeing this photograph as a child. My family must have come into possession of the heirloom, but why? Were they part of this feud too?"

Sophie held Oliver's hand, "We have more questions now than answers, but what's clear is that we need to solve this mystery. Not just for us but for the sake of Whistlewood. This heirloom has divided people for too long."

Oliver nodded, picking up the amulet and holding it up to the light. "You're right, Sophie. And I think the first step is to announce its discovery. If this heirloom really does bring prosperity to the vineyards, maybe its return can heal old wounds."

"But who do we give it back to?" Sophie questioned. "The Gardiners or the McAllisters?"

Oliver looked deep into Sophie's eyes, "That, my love, is the mystery we need to solve, and quickly. The Wine and Whimsy event is just around the corner."

Sophie felt a mixture of apprehension and excitement. The mystery was unfolding, and they were at its epicenter. What they didn't know was that their lives and the fate of Whistlewood's vineyards were about to be irrevocably intertwined.

With the amulet in Oliver's hand and a sense of shared resolve, they left the attic, unaware that Thor and Luna had already embarked on a new investigative adventure of their own—following the scent of old grapevines that permeated the attic air.

The attic door closed with a soft click, sealing in it the secrets of the past and the newfound mission for the future.

The Wine and Whimsy festival was in full swing. Twinkling fairy lights adorned the stalls, laughter filled the air, and glasses clinked in a toast to good times. At the heart of it all was Sophie's flower-infused wines, a hit sensation that had everyone in Whistlewood talking. With flavors like Lavender Pinot and Rose Petal Rosé, the festival-goers couldn't get enough.

Sophie was behind her stall, wearing a beautiful sunflower dress that matched the floral theme, and she poured samples for eager attendees. She glanced at Oliver, who was a few stalls down, lost in conversation about the significance of terroir in winemaking—a topic he had studied extensively in preparation for the festival. Their eyes met, and they exchanged a warm, proud smile.

The mayor of Whistlewood, Mr. Harrison, approached Sophie's stall, holding up a glass of her Chrysanthemum Chardonnay. "Sophie, I must say, you've outdone yourself. These wines are a hit! They might very well become a staple of our little festival."

Sophie blushed, "Thank you, Mr. Harrison. The best reward is seeing everyone enjoy it."

As the night wore on, Oliver joined Sophie at her stall, helping her manage the overwhelming demand. When there was a brief lull, he pulled her aside. "I heard the festival committee is considering adding a new award category next year: Best Innovative Wine. They're already naming you the unofficial winner."

Sophie hugged Oliver tightly. "None of this would have been possible without your support. You were my rock when things got tough."

Before Oliver could respond, an announcement came from the stage. "Ladies and Gentlemen, it's time for the moment we've all been waiting for—the awards ceremony!"

Sophie and Oliver joined the crowd, standing at the back, their hands entwined. As various awards for best traditional wines were handed out, the host added, "We have a special recognition this year for a wine that has captured our hearts and palates. Although it's an unofficial category this year, we couldn't let the festival end without acknowledging Sophie's extraordinary flower-infused wines!"

The crowd erupted in applause. Sophie's face turned a shade redder than her Rose Petal Rosé. Oliver hugged her as she absorbed the love and recognition from her community. "See? I told you they were extraordinary," he whispered in her ear.

Just as they thought the night couldn't get any better, a messenger ran up to them, holding a small package. "Urgent delivery for Sophie and Oliver."

Puzzled, Sophie tore open the package to find a small note and a familiar gold amulet—the vineyard heirloom. The note read, "For the unity and prosperity of Whistlewood's vineyards. May this heirloom find its rightful home."

Sophie looked at Oliver, her eyes wide with amazement. "Do you think it's—"

"Time to solve another mystery? Absolutely," Oliver grinned, his eyes twinkling brighter than the fairy lights around them.

Both sensed that the heirloom's reappearance at this moment was no coincidence. It was as if the spirits of Whistlewood's past were calling on them to mend old wounds and sow seeds for a harmonious future.

But for now, they had a festival to enjoy and a relationship to celebrate. Little did they know that Thor and Luna, their faithful animal companions, had already begun another round of sleuthing, following a scent that led to the edge of the Gardiners' vineyard.

The festival ended with fireworks lighting up the sky, symbolizing not just the end of a successful event but also the sparks of mysteries and adventures yet to come.

Sophie, Oliver, Thor, and Luna found themselves gathered in their cozy living room, each couple basking in the triumphs of their respective adventures. The mantel was adorned with the festival's special recognition award that Sophie had received. Beside it sat the mysterious vineyard heirloom, an intriguing promise of mysteries yet to solve.

Sophie popped open a bottle of her award-winning Lavender Pinot. As the cork flew and the wine poured, she felt an overwhelming sense of happiness. Oliver held up his glass for a toast.

"To unity, to solving mysteries, and to the power of love," he proclaimed.

"Gee, when you put it that way, we sound like superheroes," Sophie giggled, clinking her glass against Oliver's.

At their feet, Thor and Luna also seemed to be in a celebratory mood. Thor playfully swatted a cork across the room, and Luna chased after it with youthful vigor. Upon retrieving it, she returned to Thor's side, dropping it in front of him as if offering her own toast.

Oliver grabbed a small saucer and poured a tiny amount of Sophie's Lavender Pinot into it. Thor and Luna sniffed it curiously before taking tentative sips, their tails wagging in approval.

"See? Even they agree you've created something extraordinary," Oliver remarked.

Sophie looked down at her award, back at the heirloom, and finally into Oliver's eyes. "We've both been part of something extraordinary, love. We faced adversity, discovered secrets, and came out stronger."

"Yes, we did. And we'll do it again, as many times as it takes. Together," Oliver affirmed.

, Thor started meowing and Luna began to bark, their eyes fixed on a distant corner of the room. Sophie and Oliver followed their gaze, finding nothing out of the ordinary.

"Do you think they're sensing another mystery?" Sophie asked, half-joking.

Oliver grinned. "With those two, anything is possible. Whistlewood has a way of keeping us on our toes."

Sophie snuggled closer to Oliver, comforted by his presence and the sense of unity they had found. " it's a good thing we have each other—and our little detectives."

As they settled into a loving embrace, Thor and Luna circled around them before lying down, as if forming a protective barrier around their humans. It was a perfect picture of contentment and victory, one that only those who have faced trials and emerged stronger could truly understand.

Outside, the moon shone brightly over Whistlewood, its silver glow bathing the town in a celestial light that seemed to promise more adventures, more challenges, and more opportunities for love and unity.

Tonight, however, was a night for celebration, for uncorking the bottled joys and triumphs, both big and small. And as they raised another toast, Sophie, Oliver, Thor, and Luna felt nothing but gratitude for the happiness they had found and the mysteries they had untangled.

Unbeknownst to them, a shadow flickered across the heirloom, as if acknowledging their accomplishments and silently vowing that their journey was far from over. But those were worries for another day. Tonight was about victory, love, and the beauty of a life well-lived. Cheers to that.

Whimsical Futures

Sophie sat at her kitchen table, flipping through bridal magazines and circling flower arrangements that caught her eye. Petals and bouquets filled her imagination, but her thoughts kept drifting to the look on Oliver's face when he'd proposed. She still felt the glow of the vineyard's stars on her skin, their light magnifying the sparkle of her new engagement ring.

Oliver, sitting across from her, was engrossed in a book about wedding traditions. It was just like him to dive into literature at a time like this. With reading glasses perched on his nose, he looked so endearing that Sophie couldn't resist capturing the moment with her phone.

"What are you doing?" Oliver looked up, slightly bewildered as the camera shutter clicked.

"Candid shots for our wedding memories. Can't let these little moments slip by," Sophie replied, smiling warmly at him.

Oliver chuckled. "Speaking of memories, this book mentions 'something old, something new, something borrowed, something blue.' How do you feel about incorporating those into our wedding?"

Sophie pondered for a moment. "Something old could be my grandma's locket, and something new could be my wedding dress. Something borrowed is usually from a happily married friend, so that could be Rachel's pearl earrings. And something blue...well, how about we put a blue ribbon around Thor and Luna as they walk down the aisle?"

Oliver's eyes lit up at the idea. "I love it, especially the part about Thor and Luna. They've been such big parts of our lives; it's fitting they should have a role in our wedding."

, Thor, the grey cat, leapt onto the table, purring as he nuzzled Sophie's arm. Luna, the beagle, padded over and wagged her tail, looking up expectantly.

"See? They approve," Sophie chuckled, scratching Thor behind his ears while giving Luna a gentle pat.

The room was filled with a sense of bliss, yet Sophie sensed an underlying layer of tension. She looked into Oliver's eyes, seeing a slight worry clouding them.

"Is everything alright?" she asked softly, placing her hand over his.

Oliver sighed, putting down his book. "I was just thinking about everything that's happened recently—the sabotage at the vineyard, the mysterious heirloom, the ongoing police investigation. It's a lot to process, even as we plan for something as beautiful as our wedding."

Sophie understood his concerns. Their life in Whistlewood, as idyllic as it seemed, had its complications. But those challenges had brought them closer, solidifying their partnership in ways that were both unexpected and deeply fulfilling.

"Life will always throw curveballs, Oliver. We've faced challenges before, and look where they led us—to an even stronger bond. We can't let the worries of yesterday or the uncertainties of tomorrow steal the joy of our today."

Oliver's eyes softened, his worry replaced by gratitude. "You're absolutely right, Sophie. We have each other, and that's more than enough to take on whatever comes our way."

Raising her glass of Lavender Pinot, Sophie proposed a toast. "To us, to our journey, and to the wonderful mysteries that await us."

Oliver clinked his glass against hers, echoing her sentiment. "To us, forever and always."

As they sipped their wine, they felt a profound sense of peace and excitement for the future. Thor meowed approvingly, while Luna barked in agreement, as if they too were toasting to the new chapter in their shared lives.

And so, amidst the delightful chaos of wedding planning and the complex tapestry of their experiences in Whistlewood, Sophie and Oliver found their moment of clarity—a moment that reaffirmed their love and their readiness to face any mystery, hand in hand, for the rest of their lives.

Sophie was rinsing wine glasses when Oliver walked into her kitchen carrying a basket of freshly baked muffins. The aromatic scent of blueberries and cinnamon filled the air, blending perfectly with the lingering notes of the flower-infused wines she was experimenting with.

"Thought we could use a snack," Oliver said, setting the basket on the table next to a vase filled with roses and daffodils.

"You read my mind," Sophie smiled, drying her hands on a dish towel and joining him at the table.

They enjoyed their muffins in a comfortable silence for a moment, each lost in their thoughts until Oliver broke the quiet.

"Sophie, have you ever thought about combining our talents in a business?"

Sophie looked at him, intrigued. "A business? Together?"

Oliver nodded. "Yes, exactly. A sort of boutique shop where we could sell your flower arrangements and some curated books. Maybe even offer workshops or wine tastings. The possibilities could be endless."

Sophie's eyes sparkled at the idea. She'd been toying with the thought of expanding her floral design business but hadn't considered bringing in Oliver's love for literature.

"I love it. Your book knowledge, my floral arrangements, and maybe even some of my experimental wines. It sounds so... harmonious."

"Harmonious. I like that," Oliver said, scribbling the word down in his ever-present notebook. "It's the perfect blend of our worlds. A place where culture and nature meet."

Sophie sipped her wine thoughtfully. "And it would be ours. A project, a life, together."

"Exactly. But it wouldn't be without challenges," Oliver cautioned, always the realist. "Location, business plans, startup capital—there's a lot to think about."

Sophie leaned in, capturing his gaze. "Oliver, we've faced vineyard saboteurs, deciphered riddles, and solved mysteries with the help of a cat and a dog. I think we can handle starting a small business."

Oliver chuckled. "When you put it like that, how could I argue?"

, Luna trotted over, her tail wagging, followed closely by Thor, who hopped up on a chair like the dignified feline he was.

"See? Even our furry little family agrees," Sophie said, stroking Luna's ears.

Oliver jotted down more notes, his eyes brimming with ideas. "We'll need to plan, strategize, research. There'll be licenses, permits, and—"

Sophie cut him off with a gentle kiss. "Yes, to all of that. But for now, let's just enjoy this moment and dream a little. We've got the rest of our lives to plan, my love."

As Oliver closed his notebook and set it aside, Sophie felt an overwhelming sense of completeness wash over her. This venture was more than just a business; it was a lifetime project that they would build together, echoing their love and shared passions.

A mysterious knock at the door interrupted their tender moment.

"Who could that be?" Oliver wondered aloud, rising to answer it.

Sophie's heart skipped a beat. After all they'd been through, any unexpected visitor could mean another twist in their always-eventful life in Whistlewood.

Oliver opened the door to find an envelope on the doormat. No person in sight. He picked it up and glanced at Sophie, a familiar sparkle of curiosity lighting his eyes.

Sophie felt a thrill of excitement. It looked like their next adventure was about to begin, but whatever lay ahead, she knew they would face it together. Business partners, life partners, and the best of friends—Sophie and Oliver were ready for anything.

As Sophie and Oliver opened the mysterious envelope, Thor and Luna perked up, sensing the excitement and tension in the room. Oliver unfolded the paper and read the note aloud, a string of seemingly nonsensical symbols and numbers.

"Well, this doesn't make much sense, does it?" Oliver commented, setting the note on the table.

Sophie squinted at the paper. "It looks like a code of some sort."

, Luna hopped up on the table, her nose twitching as she sniffed at the note. Thor joined her, his eyes scanning the mysterious symbols. It was as if they were reading it, each in their own way.

Sophie chuckled. "Look at them, so intrigued. It's like they want to crack the code themselves."

Oliver joined in her laughter. "Well, they are experienced detectives by now."

They watched as Thor sat back, staring at the note with his deep green eyes, almost as if he was pondering the meaning of the symbols. Luna, not to be outdone, pawed at the paper and sat, staring at her human parents, her tail wagging in excitement.

"Should we be concerned that our pets seem better at decoding than we are?" Sophie joked.

Oliver picked up the note and walked over to his bookshelf, pulling out a book on cryptography. "Maybe they're on to something. Let me see here..."

As he leafed through the pages, Sophie noticed Thor and Luna sharing a glance, almost as if they were communicating silently. Luna let out a soft "woof," and Thor responded by swatting gently at the note, knocking it closer to Luna.

Sophie watched in disbelief as Luna took the edge of the note in her mouth and gently placed it on the floor, right in front of a small toy piano that belonged to Thor. The cat gracefully walked over to the piano and tapped a few keys with his paw.

"Are you seeing this?" Sophie said, her eyes widening.

"Seeing it and not believing it," Oliver responded, putting down his book to watch the pets.

Thor tapped a series of keys that surprisingly mimicked the sequence of symbols on the note. As the last note rang out, Luna let out a joyful bark.

Sophie and Oliver looked at each other, stunned. Then, almost automatically, Oliver reached for his notebook and jotted down the sequence of musical notes that Thor had just played.

"Sophie, I think our pets just decoded this message. Each symbol represents a musical note."

Sophie grabbed her phone and started inputting the notes into a music app. When played back, it was a melody, and hidden within it were a series of tones that sounded eerily like Morse code.

Oliver quickly decoded it: "The treasure is hidden where the sun kisses the vines."

Both Sophie and Oliver looked at each other, eyes wide with wonder and a touch of disbelief. their gaze shifted to Thor and Luna, who sat side by side, looking extremely pleased with themselves.

Sophie leaned over to give Luna a big hug while Oliver scratched Thor behind his ears.

"Looks like we're not the only mystery-solving duo in this family," Sophie said, smiling at Oliver.

"And it seems like our next adventure is right around the corner," he added, gripping the decoded note in his hand.

As they embraced, Luna barked and Thor let out a pleased meow, both animals eagerly awaiting the new adventures that surely lay ahead. The family they had formed—two humans, a cat, and a dog—felt complete, ready to face any mystery, any challenge, as long as they were together.

And so, the promise of another adventure lingered in the air, like the last note of a beautiful, unfinished symphony.

The Twinkle in the Wine

Sophie and Oliver sat in the cozy living room of their Whistlewood home, a space filled with the aroma of lavender and the gentle melody of classical music streaming from the gramophone. A bottle of Sophie's acclaimed flower-infused wine was uncorked and poured into two glasses that sat on the coffee table.

"To the future," Oliver raised his glass.

"And to love," Sophie added, tapping her glass against his in a sparkling toast.

As they each took a sip, their eyes met, and they shared a moment of contentment, each recalling the whirlwind of mysteries, challenges, and emotions that had led them to this blissful point.

The room was filled with the comforts that made their house a home. On one wall was Oliver's collection of literary classics and mysteries, their spines showing signs of frequent use. On the opposite wall, near the window, stood Sophie's worktable, where she designed her floral arrangements. It was chaotic and messy in an artistic way, with sketches of arrangements, a myriad of colorful ribbons, and jars of various flower essences.

Their eyes met again, and Oliver broke the silence. "So, we really should start thinking about wedding plans, shouldn't we?"

Sophie's eyes twinkled. "Oh, absolutely. I've been thinking of a spring wedding. You know, when the cherry blossoms are in full bloom. What do you think?"

"I think it would be perfect. Just like you," Oliver said, leaning in for a kiss.

As their lips met, Luna, the beagle, trotted into the room, tail wagging, followed by Thor, the grey cat, whose eyes narrowed as he leapt gracefully onto a chair, settling himself like a king overseeing his kingdom.

Sophie chuckled. "They are so different, and yet they fit together so well. Kind of like us."

"Exactly like us," Oliver affirmed. "And speaking of fitting together, I've been considering something."

"Oh?" Sophie leaned in, curious.

"What do you think of combining our talents into a business? A sort of boutique that offers both books and floral creations? We could call it 'Blooms & Tomes' or something like that."

Sophie's eyes widened with excitement. "Oh, Oliver, that's a brilliant idea! I can already imagine how it would look. Half of the store filled with the scents of fresh flowers, and the other half with the intoxicating aroma of old books."

"I knew you'd like it," Oliver said with a grin. "And think of the mysteries we could solve with a store as our base of operations!"

Sophie laughed. "True, it seems like Whistlewood never has a shortage of those."

, Luna let out a soft "woof," and Thor responded with a purr, almost as if agreeing with their humans.

"See, even our furry detectives are on board with the idea," Sophie said, petting Luna's head as she leaned against her leg.

Thor jumped off the chair and padded over to Oliver, who picked him up and settled him on his lap. "Well, then, it's unanimous."

As they sat there, two couples in one room, both different and yet so alike, Sophie felt a warm rush of happiness wash over her.

"To our future, our family, and our upcoming adventures," Oliver raised his glass again.

"To all of it," Sophie concurred, feeling in her heart that they were at the threshold of a new, exciting chapter in their lives.

They clinked their glasses one more time, sealing their pact, while Luna and Thor settled in, sensing that life was about to get even more interesting. It was a beautiful evening, one that hinted at the countless beautiful days to come.

Thor and Luna watched with curious eyes as Sophie headed into the kitchen and opened the pantry. The feline and canine detectives had developed quite a sixth sense when it came to their favorite part of the day—treat time.

Sophie reached into separate jars labeled "Thor's Delights" and "Luna's Munchies." She took out a small, fish-shaped cat treat for Thor and a bone-shaped biscuit for Luna. Returning to the living room, she noticed Oliver setting aside his tablet, which was opened to an article on the complexities of small business ownership.

Sophie knelt and offered the treats to the pets. Luna wagged her tail and gulped down her biscuit with gusto. Thor, with feline dignity, sniffed his fish-shaped treat before nibbling it delicately.

"They've earned this," Sophie said, sitting back on the couch beside Oliver.

"They've more than earned it," Oliver agreed, stroking Thor's gray fur as the cat jumped up onto his lap. "These two have been instrumental in solving our little town's mysteries. They're the unsung heroes of Whistlewood."

Sophie chuckled as Luna nudged her, asking for a belly rub. "I don't think they're completely unsung. Remember Mrs. Higgins' poem at the last Whistlewood meeting?"

Oliver laughed, recalling the eccentric townswoman's heartfelt but somewhat rambling ode to the 'Furry Protectors of Whistlewood.' "True, but a little more recognition wouldn't hurt. Maybe they can be the honorary mascots for 'Blooms & Tomes.'"

Sophie clapped her hands together. "Oh, that's a fabulous idea! Think about it, their cute faces on our store's sign, website, and even merchandise! And, of course, they'll have their own corner in the store."

"A cozy nook filled with the finest pet treats and cushions," Oliver imagined aloud. "They've certainly earned their keep, and some."

Sophie grew thoughtful for a moment. "You know, I often wonder what sort of adventures they have when we're not looking."

Oliver smirked. "I wouldn't be surprised if they've solved more mysteries than we're aware of."

, Thor began purring loudly, as if in agreement, while Luna let out a playful bark. Both pets sauntered off to their respective cozy spots in the room. Luna curled up in her soft, padded dog bed, while Thor leapt onto the window sill, looking out into the night as if contemplating his next great adventure.

Sophie and Oliver exchanged glances, both sensing that their pets were far more perceptive and mysterious than they let on.

"Here's to our unsung heroes," Oliver lifted his wine glass toward the pets.

Sophie joined him, raising her glass. "And to the many more adventures we'll undoubtedly share."

They clinked glasses, and as they did, both Thor and Luna seemed to look their way for just a moment, as if acknowledging their human's tribute. It was a simple but meaningful family ritual, one that bound them together in anticipation of the unknown adventures that lay ahead.

"We're a family of detectives and dreamers, aren't we?" Sophie mused.

Oliver looked at her, at their pets, and smiled. "Yes, and I couldn't imagine a better team to navigate whatever comes next."

And so, as they enjoyed their evening, the line between the human world and the pet world seemed to blur just a little, merging their destinies as co-adventurers and as a family, forever intertwined.

Sophie sat at her antique vanity, thumbing through an album filled with photos of her and Oliver, as well as snapshots capturing their adventures with Thor and Luna. The pictures told the story of not just a love blossoming between two humans, but also a heartwarming tale of a feline and a canine becoming the best of friends, and heroes to boot.

Oliver walked in, setting down a book he had been perusing on the business prospects for Whistlewood, their future joint venture in literary and floral beauty.

"Reminiscing, are we?" he said softly, wrapping his arms around Sophie's shoulders from behind and peering into the mirror at their reflections.

"Yes," Sophie sighed. "It's just astounding how much we've all been through. The mysteries we've solved, the difficulties we've overcome. We've really made a life here, haven't we?"

Oliver smiled, looking into her eyes through the mirror. "We have, and it's just the beginning."

Sophie closed the album and stood, taking a moment to scratch Luna, who had lazily wandered into the room, behind her ears. Luna responded with a wag of her tail and a contented bark. Thor, who had been leisurely stretched out on the windowsill, rose and stretched himself, as if acknowledging the importance of the moment.

"As much as I'm excited about 'Blooms & Tomes', and our wedding, and everything else," Sophie started, "I also feel like Thor and Luna have their own paths to explore. Do you ever think about what they'd do if they weren't with us?"

Oliver chuckled. "Honestly, I think they'd be leading some sort of pet resistance movement against errant squirrels. Or perhaps they'd be the Sherlock Holmes and Dr. Watson of the animal kingdom."

Sophie laughed, picking up Thor who had leapt down from the windowsill to join them. "You know, Mrs. Miggins from the bakery told me she's been hearing strange noises at night. She thinks her shop might be haunted by the ghost of her predecessor, Old Man Higgins."

Oliver raised an eyebrow. "Well, sounds like another job for our dynamic duo here," he said, nodding toward Thor and Luna.

Sophie set Thor down, and he immediately sauntered over to Luna, nudging her playfully. Luna barked, and the two pets scampered out of the room as if sensing another adventure on the horizon.

Sophie and Oliver shared a knowing glance and held each other close. Their journey had started as two separate paths that not only intertwined but created a tapestry of shared experiences and adventures, ones both known and yet to be discovered. They had not only found love but had also become a part of something larger—a community, a network of friends, and a partnership that extended beyond just business.

As they stood there, contemplating their past and future, the couple knew one thing was certain: Whatever came next, they would face it together, as a family.

Sophie looked deeply into Oliver's eyes. "Here's to our next chapter, and many more."

Oliver kissed her passionately. "And to the countless adventures that await."

Unseen by them, a piece of paper slipped from Oliver's book and floated gently to the ground. On it was a list of odd occurrences reported in Whistlewood, complete with a small drawing of a paw and a whisker—the unofficial signature of their unsung heroes.

The adventures were far from over, and in that quiet moment, the promise of future mysteries filled the air, keeping the spirit of Whistlewood, and its guardian couples, very much alive.

Made in the USA
Columbia, SC
07 November 2023

25125278R00048